MERLOT

REBELLION

Leigh Jarrett

Published by Steambath Press
An LJ Gay Romance

Paperback published April 2023
ISBN-13: 978-1-998008-04-9

Chapter One | Patrick

A gorgeous sunny sky with a light breeze that took the sweltering heat off his skin. The boat in motion across the calm blue water. Laughter coming from the latest group of tourists Patrick was taking out on a cruise around the central part of Okanagan Lake.

Life was good.

They had taken off from Kelowna Downtown Marina in the interior of British Columbia, Canada. An immense, deep lake surrounded by many sandy and stony shores. Patrick had grown up there. It was all he knew. He'd only ever been up and down the Okanagan Valley. He'd never even made it to Vancouver on the west coast. In some small way, he was proud of that.

To the south, the semi-arid shrubland of South Okanagan received the brunt of the summer heat, boasting the title of the only desert in Canada. To the north, the scenery became a bit greener. The Shuswap: rainy seasons and plenty of snow created a haven for evergreen forests.

Patrick turned the boat north away from the bridge so his group for the afternoon could see the cityscape, sparse as it was, bordering the lake. Then he traveled across the lake to the west. There were some big houses the tourists always enjoyed peering at from the water. A bit of voyeurism was always on the agenda. He smiled as the group oohed and aahed at the luxury homes.

Next, he headed south and under the bridge. A section of the bridge's significant length was floating. Part of it was high enough for boats to travel under. They cruised down the lake, toward a small dot of land in the water called Rattlesnake Island. It had an unusual history. Patrick loved telling the story. It was always a crowd-pleaser amongst tourists and residents alike.

"On your left, you'll see Rattlesnake Island." Patrick slowed the engine. "By all accounts, it's not called that because it has rattlesnakes. Although, there might be a few. As for creatures, it is said to be the home of the Ogopogo. The Okanagan's very own legendary monster."

A collective, "Ah," drifted toward him. People held up their phones and took pictures of the mundane-looking lump of rock.

"Back in the 1970s, it was owned by businessman, Eddie Haymour. He had dreams of developing the island into an Okanagan premier entertainment attraction. It was to be Arab-themed. A mini-golf course, replica pyramids, restaurants, and a giant camel." There were a few giggles. "It didn't happen as he'd intended," Patrick added.

A robust man in plaid swim shorts and a tank top raised his hand. He was indicative of the tourists Patrick found on his tours. Summer attire. Dressed for the weather. Some from across the country. Some international. Some local. Everyone was there for a good time in the sun.

"What happened?" the man asked.

"Well. Eddie claimed the provincial government was out to get him. Even so, undeterred, he began building his theme park. You can still see remnants of it on the island. The plan was to ferry people across the lake from Peachland. It only saw seventy visitors before it shut down."

Patrick eased the boat away from the island. "He wasn't entirely wrong about the government. They went beyond their authority. Their actions resulted in the bank pulling Eddie's loans. Then the government offered to buy the island off him for a pittance of what he had sunk into it. Eventually, he signed it over." Patrick turned to face his audience. "Feeling frustrated with the treatment he had received, Haymour returned to Lebanon, and with the help of his family, he seized the Canadian embassy in Beirut. Thirty-four hostages and nine hours later, the British Columbia government agreed to discuss the case with him. He was awarded $250,000 in compensation."

"That's an insane story." A woman in a bright, flowery dress took another photo of the island, then sat down. She was right. It was quite the story for a worthless piece of nondescript land that blended into the background of the mountains behind it. You could easily miss it.

Everyone seated; Patrick increased his speed. This side of the lake was always choppier. He wasn't sure why. But skipping over the rough waves made for a fun ride.

He headed back north. They had one last stop to make. Close to the city, before the bridge, there was a bank of sand under the waves that extended quite far out before dropping off into the abyss. Patrick slowed the boat, lifted the propeller, drifted, then dropped anchor.

"Anyone want to take a dip? The water out here is only chest high."

A few people climbed off the back of the boat into the water: little sighs of delight as they discovered he was telling the truth about the depth of water. The water was warmer here, but cooler than the surrounding air. It was a scorching hot August afternoon. Typical for the time of year but Patrick was used to it. Even so, once he brought this tour back, he was going to spend some time in the water himself. The company he worked for also rented out jet skis. A spin around the lake on one of those was a great way to cool off. Then maybe a quick dip.

Then back home to his empty apartment.

Patrick gripped the steering wheel. Two months had passed since his boyfriend of two years had kicked him out. Aubrey Leroy Schatzki. The guy he had thought he was going to spend more than two years with. Not an eternity with. They weren't *that* compatible. But it had been a comfortable relationship. He'd been in love with Aubrey. Not desperate hard, though.

Again—it was just comfortable.

It had been the latest in a string of failed relationships. As soon as he felt like he was falling in love, a deal breaker would appear. Either the guy was anti-trans, crazy right-wing—or not looking for anything long-term serious. Aubrey had assured him he wasn't any of those things. He'd talked of wanting to get married at some point in his life and creating a family with children.

He'd said all the right things. After a year together, Patrick moved in with Aubrey. He wasn't convinced Aubrey was *the one*, but he was willing to give it a try.

Getting kicked out suddenly—that had been a shocker.

Patrick's tourists scurried back aboard and grabbed their towels, accompanied by excited conversations about what a lovely afternoon it had been. He brought them back under the bridge and approached the marina, pulled the boat into the dock, leaped out to tether it, and reminded everyone to leave their lifejackets with the front desk as they filed past him.

As he walked the dock toward the office, he adjusted his hair in the knot on top of his head he wore to keep the length out of his face. The summer sun had turned his blond hair almost white in places. If it was down, it would hang past his shoulders; a cascading, golden display only his lovers had the pleasure of experiencing. He smirked as he headed to the rental kiosk.

He'd had many of those in the past two months. Lovers. He handed the keys for the boat over to the guy manning the office and slipped a set for one of the jet skis off a hook.

Amenable men were scarce in a small town, so he'd revisited guys he had slept with before. There was comfort in familiarity. Some gay—some straight. A couple of them were friends. It was casual. No expectations. Aubrey had burned him bad. He wasn't ready for another relationship.

He was still licking his wounds.

Patrick fired up the jet ski and took off across the lake. The spray of cold water and crazy speed gave him the relief he had been craving all afternoon. This was freedom; being out on the water. He flew and swerved back and forth across the water at the base of the city.

He laughed and whooped as he completed a figure-eight, refreshing water spraying everywhere. His heart was thundering. His soul in flight. He slowed his speed. He was going to be fried to a crisp by the time he got back. His sunscreen had long since worn off.

Shifting from his usual carefree self, Patrick headed back to the marina. After checking his schedule for the next week, he wandered over to his beat-up Ford F150 Ranger. It had seen better days. Long before he owned it. He was lucky to have any wheels at all.

Work was hard to come by in the winter months. The city practically shuttered when the tourists left. He had opted to stick with bartending in the off-season, something he had done as he worked his way through university. He'd still ended up with insane student loans. He could only find part-time work during both seasons for his two different jobs, so he was always broke.

The truck's gears ground as he shifted into first. The bucket of rust was slow to accelerate. Luckily, he didn't have far to go—fifteen minutes tops. Nothing was far in Kelowna. He rented a small bachelor suite in Rutland. Not ideal as locations went but it did the trick. Having Aubrey suddenly tell him he had to get out had left him scrambling for accommodation.

It had been understood that the townhouse was Aubrey's. He'd been there for over ten years. Patrick never would have been able to afford the rent on his own anyway. It was in the Mission and way beyond his price range. Aubrey had covered the full rent during the year they had lived together. Shifting back to a modest accommodation and lifestyle had been an adjustment.

Patrick pulled into the parking lot of his apartment building and shut down his truck. He just sat there for a moment. It had come out of nowhere, the break-up. He had come home one day to find most of his clothing in the front entry. It had floored him. Aubrey *had* been pulling away for sure. But to the point of breaking up with him? He'd run up the stairs to confront Aubrey.

"I just don't love you anymore."

The words still rang in his ears.

Patrick leaned his head against the headrest. It was going to be hard to love again. To invest so much emotion in another person. Fully believe they loved you too. To put his heart out there to be handled by a guy he had feelings for. For the time being love equaled eventual heartbreak.

He climbed out of his truck and headed for the stairs up to his sparse little apartment. It was barely furnished. A bed, a table—one chair, and a ragged sofa. Plus a few things he'd picked up at thrift stores since he moved in. Most of what he had owned before moving in with Aubrey had been given to charity because he couldn't afford the cost of storage.

Plus, he hadn't thought he'd be out on his ear a mere one year later.

Aubrey hadn't given him any additional reasons for breaking things off with him. Had he done anything wrong? No. Was there anything he could have done? No. Was there someone else?

Silence.

As to whether Aubrey had ever actually loved him. It was debatable.

Patrick sighed.

He should have expected it. He had been Aubrey's quick rebound off a long-term relationship. Aubrey had struck up a friendship with him. He had thought it was that innocent at the time. A month later they started dating. A year after that, they'd moved in together.

Looking back, there was a possibility Aubrey had been seeing both him and his long-term ex-partner at the same time in the first few months. He never would have started dating Aubrey if he'd even suspected he was still with his partner of seven years.

A partner that was a nightmare. The stories Aubrey had told him … it sounded like Aubrey's ex-boyfriend was a monster. Cold, controlling—manipulative. Cruel. Story after story, Patrick had soon come to hate the boyfriend Aubrey had endured for years.

It was no wonder Aubrey had wanted out.

But to go so far as to cheat on the guy. Patrick tipped his head back and forth and stretched out the muscles in his neck that had been held tight while gripping the handlebars of the jet ski.

Honestly, after two years with him, he wouldn't put it past Aubrey to have found someone else to replace him too. He was too slick. Too socially adept. Too charming.

Too fucking gorgeous.

Guys like him had it easy. They had a lot to offer. As a real estate agent, Aubrey didn't need to be renting. He was rolling in it. He just hadn't found the right property yet. What Aubrey had been doing with a summer tour boat operator and part-time bartender like him was anyone's guess.

And yet, Aubrey had seen something in him. Or maybe he had just been a distraction. He hated to believe that. Aubrey had said he loved him. His heart couldn't stand for that not to be true. Despite the casual nature of their relationship, he'd invested a lot of emotion into it.

It hurt to think those two years had been a farce.

Patrick flicked on the lights over the kitchenette. He'd picked up some broccoli the day before. That and rice would have to do for dinner tonight. He kicked aside a cola box, pulled the hotplate out from under the cabinets, found a pot, filled it with water, and placed it on the element. After measuring out two cups of rice into the water, he turned it on high.

He couldn't stay mad at Aubrey. Crazy as it was, Patrick held no animosity against him. His inability to truly love wasn't entirely his fault. His previous relationship had damaged him.

Patrick had never met the ex-boyfriend. Sure, he knew of him. It was a small town. But they ran in different circles. The times he had spotted him, he was the sullen, brooding guy hanging back and barely interacting with his friends except when it came to tossing money around and paying for everyone's drinks. Then his dark eyes would glisten while listening to the accolades.

He didn't consider himself part of the crowd. He held court.

Everyone in his circle was beneath him.

Charles.

The guy was an asshole—plain and simple.

Chapter Two | Charles

The morning had been rushed. One problem after another had presented itself. Nothing was coming together as it should. The winemaker was complaining about staffing in the winery, despite the hiring fair they'd put together. Experienced cellar hands were hard to come by in such a small and competitive market. On top of that, the hospitality manager had reported the head chef had called in sick and the sous chef was new and hadn't mastered the menu.

Charles ran a hand through his hair. They were going to have to rely on the longstanding line cooks to keep things running smoothly in the restaurant. It was the least of his worries. Not even on his list of responsibilities for the day. Delegating was the only way he managed it all.

Quail's Run Winery was his life. Most days, Charles ran it like a well-calibrated clock. But he'd bumped into his ex-boyfriend in the tasting room, and it had rattled him. *Boyfriend*—they'd been so much more than that. They'd been together for over seven years. They'd been partners.

Aubrey Leroy Schatzki. The love of his life. The man he had imagined spending the rest of his life with. The man that had broken his heart over two years ago.

Charles released a sigh and returned his mind to his job. Today was cram-packed full of things to do. He had a meeting with the marketing manager to analyze their target audiences and see if they couldn't figure out some inroads into new markets.

That and the website was out of date. It should have been tackled in the spring, but the marketing manager was new and was still getting his feet wet. They would need to brainstorm how they could quickly improve it for the summer tourist season. The wine-tasting room and restaurant were already crowded daily, with wine tour buses arriving regularly. But more was better.

The patio and walk were full of people taking pictures of the vineyards. The vines were full and plump with grapes. The harvest season was about to begin. It ran from mid-August through to October. Except for the rows they left on the vine to be harvested in January for ice wine.

Charles rebuttoned the coat of his suit jacket.

That was his morning. This afternoon was a meeting with the accountant. Not his favorite. But numbers came easy to him. Spreadsheets were a breeze. It was dull stuff compared to the excitement of actual winemaking. He'd practically grown up in a winery. His dad had owned a small family winery on the other side of the lake. As a teenager, he had been sent out to pick grapes and prune vines. He felt like he'd become an expert at both. On not such good days, he had endured the dreaded tasks of cleaning the cellars and bottling wine.

"Charles." The sous chef handed him a sheet of paper. A menu. "I've made a few changes to the menu to hold us through until Chef is back on his feet. I've scaled it back so I can manage it."

Charles perused what had been reduced to a slim offering of food options. It wasn't good enough. Their patrons would expect more from them. The sous chef really should have brought it to the hospitality manager. Not someone so high up the food chain. This decision was beyond the scope of his position. But the guy had brought it to him, and Charles wasn't happy with it.

"This won't do. Stick to the regular menu." He handed the paper back to the sous chef. "I appreciate your initiative, but if you're lost, ask one of the people who have been here longer."

"Yes, sir."

The look of defeat on the sous chef's face almost had Charles changing his mind. But he wouldn't compromise. It was going to be a sink-or-swim day for the new guy.

He checked the time on his phone and headed for his office. He had a few phone calls to make. Plus, he needed to be away from people for a few minutes. He burned out easily, mentally. Not a great trait to have when your job was dealing with people. But he loved the challenge of it. Balancing and driving an incredible group of people and bringing their wines to the world.

Charles relaxed into the chair behind his desk. Seeing Aubrey today had not helped with the stress load he was under. Aubrey knew better than to visit his winery. They had agreed he wouldn't come near the place. He had arrived with an entourage of his visitors. But no boyfriend. Charles had heard through the queer grapevine that Aubrey had broken up with his vapid boy toy.

He still couldn't believe Aubrey had left him for a lazy, insipid beach bum. By all accounts, Charles and Aubrey had been happy. Sure, they had their problems. Both of their schedules created few opportunities for them to hang out with each other. Have date nights. Discuss issues. Their lives hadn't been perfect. In fact, Charles often found himself going out with friends on his own.

Much like he did now.

He wasn't sure why he did it. Headed out with friends. The crowds of people always overstimulated him. He tried to hold back, to protect his anxiety level by keeping to himself, but it often didn't work. Shy didn't touch on how awkward he could be with people outside of work.

Work was different. He could put on a costume of sorts. General manager of a mid-sized, very profitable winery. He could play that role. And he played it well.

But with Aubrey, that was a role he hadn't played well. He had tried to be attentive. Caring and understanding. But Aubrey was broken. Love didn't come easy for him.

Charles wiped a stray tear from his cheek. The day Aubrey had come home and asked him to move out—it had devastated him.

"I just don't love you anymore."

The words still rang in his ears.

It reminded him of when his mom had left his dad for another man. He remembered standing there in the front entry at the age of nine; his mom telling his dad she didn't love him anymore. That she loved someone else. That he wasn't good enough. That she was leaving him.

Charles hadn't been with anyone since Aubrey. Dated or slept with. He was convinced he wasn't good enough for anyone either. That he was damaged. The shyness—the anxiety. The crippling self-doubt he suffered from. He knew that if he went out with someone for long enough, they'd eventually figure it out. Know he was no good. Dump him—and break his heart.

Aubrey had turned him out after stripping away every bit of confidence he had. Their time together had been toxic. He knew that now. But to find out Aubrey had been seeing another guy behind his back? That the guy was some party boy many years younger than him. It had crushed him. Seven years had been thrown away for the chance to tap some young, beach-blond ass.

Every time he saw the home wrecker, he was laughing without a care in the world like he hadn't torn someone's world apart.

Patrick.

The guy was an asshole—plain and simple.

Chapter Three | Patrick

The phone rang before he was fully awake. The sun had already been streaming through his blinds making it impossible to sleep late. The added sound of the Jaws ringtone pulled him off his pillow.

Patrick reached for his phone. It was a guy he worked with, Derek.

"Hey, what's up?"

"Dude … I've got a problem."

Derek always had one problem or another. Usually, he was running late.

"I'm not working today."

"I know. I know. That's why you can help me."

Patrick swung his legs off the bed and stretched out his back.

"What do you want?"

"Dude, I have this job for you. I already cleared it with the manager. Told her how good you are with tourists. That you're crazy about wine. And you're a stand-up guy."

Patrick switched the phone to his other ear and dug around in his bedside drawer for a pen and paper. This sounded interesting. Some extra money was always welcome.

"What's the job?"

"Kind of like a wine tour guide."

"Kind of? How on earth did you land a job like that?"

"I might have lied about a few things. Thought better of it this morning."

"This morning … I need to do this today?"

"The bus leaves at ten."

Patrick pushed a couple of things aside and slapped the pad of paper he had found down on the top of the bedside table, pen poised, ready to write down some details.

"Where do I have to be?"

"The Kanada Hotel. You can't miss which bus. It's covered in pictures of wine bottles."

"And they're expecting me. You're sure?"

"Yeah, dude. It's all set."

Patrick was about to ask Derek what was required of him. What a guide did exactly. But decided against it. Chances were Derek had no idea.

"Thanks, buddy. Appreciate the reference."

"Happy drinking." Derek snorted out a laugh, then ended the call.

Patrick immediately switched to a search screen on his phone. *What does a wine tour guide do?* The results were varied. It was basically like the tour boat gig. Except he'd be talking about wine and the wineries they were visiting.

He flopped down on his back on the bed. This was going to be an adventure. Luckily, he knew loads about most of the wineries in the region. Wine was a hobby of his. Okay, more than a hobby—a bit of an obsession. It was Aubrey's fault. After two years with him, Patrick knew his way around complexity, balance, typicity, intensity, and finish.

Patrick rolled off the bed onto his feet. He texted Derek, asked for the name of the tour company, and made a quick phone call to the manager. He confirmed what was expected of him. Where to be. Where he was going. How he was being paid.

Derek had been right about the starting point. And yes, he would need his knowledge of the wineries and wines of the region. And a sense of humor. He had both covered. The tour would be visiting wineries on both sides of the lake. The driver would pay him cash.

There would be a drag queen on board.

That last detail made him feel so much better. A drag queen would be kindred folk to volley and joke with. It was very likely he already knew her. He didn't feel so alone.

After a quick breakfast of Fruit Loops, he changed into his running gear. The contradiction: junk food and exercise was the story of his life. Flipping back and forth between fun and responsibility. It's what made him so popular. His ability to switch into party mode at the drop of a hat. He checked his phone. It was still early. In another hour or so, it would be too hot to run.

He slipped his water bottle into his fanny pack and clipped the belt around his waist. The wave of heat that welcomed him as he stepped out through the door reminded him of how little time he had. An hour would have to do it. That would give him enough time to shower, have a quick nap, and meet the tour bus. Maybe brush up on a few facts about the history of winemaking in the Okanagan Valley. His mind was whirring with ideas. He would sort through everything as he ran.

As Patrick jogged down the street and headed for a trail that ran the length of a wide creek, he paged through the wines that were indicative of each region of the valley in his mind. Syrah in Oliver and Osoyoos. Merlot and Cabernet along the eastern bench. Pinot Noir and Chardonnay in East Kelowna. Rieslings and Pinot Gris up and down the lake. There were others but those tended to be the seven varieties people on his boat tours often wanted to hear about.

He breathed easier. He had been talking wine for years with the boat tourists while showing them the wonders of Okanagan Lake. There was a game he played with the tour guests. He would have them point to a vineyard on the shore and he would name the winery and describe what type of grapes they grew there and the wines they produced.

He could handle this. Being a wine tour guide.

Showered and ready for whatever the rest of the day was going to throw at him, Patrick arrived twenty minutes early and took his place at the bottom of the steps to the tour bus. He had opted for cream shorts and a white button-down cotton shirt. He wanted to look professional but not suffer too badly from the heat. But judging by the arctic breeze wafting down from the inside of the bus, they were going to be treated to an air-conditioned tour.

He welcomed each guest. Took them at their word that they had tickets. Some produced paper copies of QR codes. Some showed the codes on their cell phone screens. The manager hadn't mentioned anything to him about downloading a check-in app. Their entourage consisted of two young couples, a group of five women, two single middle-aged men, and a couple of hotties.

Patrick gave the hotties a sly smile. One of the guys winked at him. He grinned. It might turn out to be an interesting tour. Perhaps, an après tour was in his future for the evening.

He checked his phone. They were still waiting for one

person.

He nearly screamed with delight as Trixie Lamour came rushing across the parking lot, her heels clacking on the pavement, her long blonde hair flying out behind her. He had known her for nearly ten years. Since he first started attending drag shows. You could tell she was already suffering from the heat. The amount of rubber she was wearing had to be suffocating.

She grabbed his shoulders. "Patrick! I didn't know you were going to be here."

"Neither did I. Last minute gig."

"Thank God, I'm not the only queer on board." She looked into the bus and climbed up on the first step. "Wait … looks like there might be more. Oh, my … hello."

Patrick followed her aboard. "I had no idea this was going to be a drag tour when I agreed to guide it. You have no idea how much better I feel."

"I've got your back, honey." Trixie clomped her way down the aisle, swaying and laughing, and introducing herself to every row of visitors. She had a few in stitches in mere moments.

Patrick positioned himself at the front of the bus. If he ducked down a bit, he could see out the windows. He should be able to judge where they were as they drove along. There was a pole to hang onto, and he could always take a seat up front if the bus started taking curves.

Trixie plopped down at the back of the bus. She was already chatting up the two men they suspected were gay. Patrick could tell they were talking about him. Trixie was probably telling them he was single and ready to mingle. A flush of color rose in his cheeks.

The bus started and he gripped the pole.

By the time they hit their fourth winery, Patrick was starting to feel a bit tipsy. An average of five wine samples at each winery, some generous overpours, and he'd easily had three full glasses of wine. He opted to sit in the front seat. They had one winery left.

Quail's Run Winery.

It was one Patrick had never visited before. Aubrey had always said it was no good. They avoided the wines it produced. He knew very little about them. He *did* know they produced Merlot. They had won awards, so they couldn't be that bad. But Aubrey had been set against them even buying bottles from Quail's Run at the liquor store. Patrick called up their website on his phone and zipped through the details of the winery as they drove the last couple of kilometers.

They pulled into the driveway. The winery complex was impressive. The acres of vines; extensive. The winery was partly log structure, partly modern steel, and glass. It was one of the more upscale buildings he'd seen on the tour. He was excited to get inside.

Patrick hopped off the bus and headed for the winery's front door. He held it open for his visitors as they crowded inside. His first job was to introduce himself to the general manager or someone in charge and thank them for the opportunity to bring their tour there. It was a bizarre formality. His visitors were already drowning in boxes of wine aboard the bus. It was likely they would be spending hundreds more at this stop.

Patrick came to a stop. Walking toward his group— Aubrey's goddamned ex. It was no wonder Aubrey avoided this particular winery. Now it all made sense.

Charles was the fucking manager.

All those nights when Aubrey had wept in his arms, recalling the abuse Charles had subjected him to during their seven years together. The gaslighting, the intimidation, the tearing down of Aubrey's self-confidence and self-respect. Years of being separated from his family and friends. Charles had controlled every aspect of Aubrey's life. It had nearly destroyed him.

Now the abuser, a man he had come to hate, stood before him.

Patrick released a long breath. He could do this. He walked straight toward Charles and held out his hand. "Hey, I'm Patrick. Thanks for letting us invade your space."

A waft of sultry scent tickled Patrick's senses. It was earthy and intriguing. Patrick wrinkled his nose. Of course, the pretentious beast wore cologne.

Charles looked Patrick up and down, a look of disgust on his face. A scowl accompanied Charles' reluctantly extended hand. "Charles. General manager."

Patrick shook and released his hand. "Sorry. I didn't know you worked here."

"I thought they only hired experienced tour guides with a modicum of knowledge."

Okay, they were jumping right into it. The insults.

"I know my stuff."

Charles crossed his arms. "Tell me about my winery."

Patrick was glad he'd had a minute to review the history of Quail's Run. "You opened in 1989. Started as a small family winery. Brought on investors in 2003 after the owner died. You're known for your Merlot. You've tried your hand at Cabernet but it's still a new market for you. Your most popular Merlot has a hint of black cherry. You oak it, so there are layers of cedar as well."

Charles released a huffed laugh through his nose.

"2004."

Patrick wrinkled his brow. It wasn't like him to forget what he'd read. Charles was flustering him. The obnoxious, pompous ass was obviously overjoyed to have nailed him on the mistake.

Charles looked at the visitors behind Patrick.

"Welcome to Quail's Run Winery. If you'll just follow me. I'll take you to the tasting room. We have some quality wines for you to try. I hope you have room on the bus for more boxes."

All said with a cheery smile.

Patrick followed along behind the group. The guy was a two-faced prick. Turning on the charm as easily as changing his clothes.

As Charles chatted with his visitors, Patrick leaned against the serving bar. He had to admit, the fruity, medium-bodied Merlot was outstanding. Purple floral and green notes. It finished fat on the palette. Even the Cabernet was better than he had expected; dark and full-bodied.

It annoyed him.

He kept an eye on Charles. He was a natural. He loved the wines his winery produced. He even had the visitors laughing at a few jokes. It made Patrick's blood boil. Behind that friendly, boyish smile lay an ogre. Aubrey had told him about all the times Charles had forbidden him from going out with him. Aubrey was expected to stay home and work. Bring home the big bucks that helped them live in luxury while Charles galivanted around with friends.

Patrick wondered if the sharp suit Charles was sporting was paid for by Aubrey's hard work. Reportedly, Charles was a clothes horse who would only wear the most expensive clothing.

He eyed what Charles was wearing. The dark blue, tailored blend of lavish cloth was cut perfectly for his body. It showed off his broad shoulders and trim waist.

A crisp white shirt with a wide collar beneath was open at his neck. His chest was tanned, adorned by a silver chain with a pendant Patrick couldn't make out.

Patrick's gaze wandered. Charles' eyes were a warm brown hiding the callousness that lay beneath them. Long elegant lashes. His cheeks were ruddy from time out in the sun. His lips were full, deep pink, and wet. He had a habit of licking them as he spoke.

Again, Patrick found himself becoming annoyed. Charles was beautiful. The lack of confidence in his own relationship with Aubrey resurfaced. What the hell had Aubrey been doing with him? Not Charles—him. He brushed a hand across the top of his hair.

Damn.

He would forgive a man that beautiful a lot of things. Patrick exhaled. Even the way Charles moved. His gracefulness was seductive. He couldn't take his eyes off the guy.

He ducked his gaze away as Charles approached him.

Charles crossed his arms. "I think I've covered everything. Just going to have one of my staff process some orders. Then you're free to go."

"Not a moment too soon." For many reasons. He'd been mesmerized by the devil incarnate. The sooner he got out of there the better.

"I don't expect to see you back," Charles said.

"Not a chance."

"Good." Charles stared at him, unblinking, his gaze boring into Patrick's soul. He could feel the burn in his toes. "Then we understand each other."

"Perfectly."

Patrick was back on the bus before the visitors even left the winery, slumped in his seat. If it wasn't for Trixie, the trip back to the hotel would have been in silence. Charles had got under his skin. He felt like he needed a shower to scrub away the intensity of the way Charles had sized him up when he first approached him in that winery. It made him feel dirty.

And not in a good way.

Chapter Four | Charles

Charles set his pen down and closed the report he was reviewing when someone rapped on his door. He looked at his phone. It was too early for his next appointment. "Come in."

The day had been full of interruptions.

In popped a face he hadn't seen in ages. Bianca Littlemore. The most fabulous fag-hag he'd ever had the pleasure of being followed around by. They'd met nine years ago. A night out dancing, and she'd latched onto him after they'd shared a few drinks. She'd moved away three years ago to Los Angeles to pursue a music career. Bianca had an incredible voice. She was sassy and she was gorgeous and bordered on being an extreme case of eccentric. Bright colors were her thing.

She burst into his office like a kaleidoscope of gaudy whirlwinds.

Charles slammed his hand on the desk, laughing.

"Would you look what the fucking cat dragged in!"

Charles pushed up out of his chair and rounded his desk to hug her. She wrapped her arms tight around his neck and kissed his cheek.

"Hello, beautiful man." Bianca released him.

"What the hell are you doing in town?" Charles sat on the edge of his desk.

"I had some business. Dad died. I'm the executor. So,

lots to do."

"I'm so sorry. I liked your dad."

"He was a charmer."

"And a damned good cook."

Bianca dropped into a chair in front of Charles' desk. "He liked you." She dug around in her purse and produced a phone. "You know a funny thing happened with this phone."

"What?"

"It stopped receiving text messages from you."

"I'm sorry. I've been busy."

"Busy with that man of yours, I suspect. How is that gorgeous beast of yours, Aubrey?"

Charles shook his head. "We're not together anymore."

"Seriously? I thought you two were headed for marriage."

"We were."

"What happened?"

"He cheated on me. Left me for the other guy."

"Jesus, Charles … I'm sorry." Bianca put her phone back in her purse. "Never liked him."

"Aubrey?"

"Yeah. I didn't like the way he treated you."

Charles sighed. "It was toxic, I know. But I was devastated when he kicked me out."

"Kicked you out?"

"He came home one day and wanted me gone. I had to scramble."

Bianca furrowed her brow. "So, who's this guy he left you for? Should we kill him?"

"They're not together anymore."

"When did all this happen?"

"Just over two years ago."

"Why didn't you reach out?"

"I didn't want to bother you with my drama."

Bianca crossed her arms. "You know I love drama." She cracked the gum she was chewing. "Tell me about this homewrecker. Must have been something special to draw Aubrey away."

Charles shook his head. "That's the thing. He's a nobody. Just some blond ass Aubrey wanted to tap for a couple of years. There was no way he meant anything to Aubrey."

"We hate him."

"With a passion." Charles rose. "Can I get you a glass of wine?"

"Thought you'd never ask." Bianca followed Charles out into the tasting room. "Maybe we could take your boat out. I'd love to get out on the water. I've had a long day."

"That can definitely be arranged. I haven't been out in a couple of weeks."

"Quick glass then we'll go?"

"Just let me move some appointments around."

After a responsible amount of wine was consumed by Charles, not so much by Bianca, they headed for the marina. Charles' boat was a slate grey and white cabin cruiser. A Tiara 43 LE. It was elegant and sophisticated. He didn't take her out as often as he would like but he kept her ready to go for when he did find a few spare hours. Sometimes he held staff parties on her.

He fired her up. The boat rumbled beneath his feet.

Charles eased her out of the marina and headed for the bridge. He'd run them to Naramata. Check out the slopes of vineyards from the water. The sight was reliably stunning. It reminded him of why he loved the wine business so much. Why he loved the Okanagan. It would take a few hours to get there and back. They could stop for dinner in Peachland.

They enjoyed the speed and the wind in silence as they made their way down the lake. Bianca leaned against his chair as he drove, a glass of wine in her hand.

"I saw him yesterday," Charles said.

"Who?"

"The vapid whore."

"The guy Aubrey cheated on you with?"

Charles nodded. "He came in with a wine tour group." He snorted. "He was leading it. Caught me completely off guard. Snide little bitch tried to get under my skin."

"Sounds like he did." Bianca touched his arm. "You need to let it go."

"I can't get it out of my head that Aubrey was sleeping with us both. He was coming home with that guy's scent on him. Crawling into our bed. Kissing me with that same mouth."

"You didn't suspect anything?"

"Sure. He was staying out more often. Missing dinner. Having more showers."

"Did you confront him?"

"You know what he was like. He made me feel like I was delusional. That I was paranoid. That I was trying to control him. That it was all my fault he was staying away from home."

"I don't know how you stayed with him as long as you did."

"It's not all his fault. I'm responsible too. I wasn't easy to live with."

"I find that impossible to believe."

"Dammit." Charles slowed the boat as the rumble of the engine cut in and out. The damned thing was going to stall. The engine roared and then went silent. The inertia of the speed they'd been going at rocked the boat forward. Then back and forth until it was still in the water. It rolled side to side on the current. Charles headed down the steps onto the deck.

"What happened?" Bianca asked as she followed him.

"Not sure. She's been acting up recently."

"What do we do?"

"I'll get a hold of someone."

Charles pulled out his phone and put a call into the marina. The guy he spoke to said it would take them an hour to reach their location.

"Now we wait." He reclined in one of the seats. "Any more wine?"

"You're well stocked below. I'll grab you a glass."

Charles sighed and relaxed. It wasn't so bad. Sitting there in the silence of the lake. No boat noises. No jet skis. Just the sound of water lapping up against the side of the boat.

He took the glass offered to him and turned his face to the sun. Bianca stretched out on the bench seating. It was a pleasant way to spend the afternoon.

The quiet was interrupted sooner than he'd been expecting.

A boat rumbled to starboard.

Charles opened his eyes. He clenched his fist and set his glass down. There at the wheel of the boat beside them was the adulteress. Charles rose to his feet. The last thing he needed was help from the guy who'd wrecked his life. The hatred ran far too deep.

"We're fine," Charles called.

"So, you're drifting on purpose," Patrick said.

Charles rolled his eyes. *Fuck.* He'd forgotten to drop anchor. He'd been flustered. Now his ears were burning. The little blond tramp probably thought this was pretty funny.

So, he lied.

"I'm having trouble with the anchor."

"Do you want me to take a look at it?"

Over my dead body.

He didn't want the guy anywhere near his boat. "No, I'll wait for the guy the marina sent."

Patrick crossed his arms. "You're looking at him." He pointed at Charles' boat. "I'm going to have to come aboard if you want my help."

"I'd rather drift."

Patrick shrugged. "Suit yourself. You might change your mind when it gets dark, and you run aground out here in the middle of nowhere."

Bianca touched Charles' shoulder. "What's going on?"

"That's the guy," Charles said over his shoulder.

"Aubrey's guy?" She took a sip of her wine. "He's cute."

Charles turned and stared at her. "Bianca. You're not helping."

"What? He is."

"If you don't want me on board," Patrick said. "I could just tow you."

The anger and frustration rolled in Charles' gut. The chance of anyone else coming their way and helping them was slim. This might be their only chance to get out of there. The thought of being towed by this guy infuriated him. Better to have him look at the boat.

"Fine." Charles swept his arm out, giving Patrice permission to come aboard.

Patrick dropped his own anchor and jumped onto Charles' boat. He turned the key on the driving console. He snorted out a laugh. "It helps to fill your boat with gas before you go out."

The color that flushed Charles' face burned his ears. This was beyond humiliating. Part of the service he paid for at the marina; they would always make sure his boat was full of gas.

He hadn't even thought to check.

"I haven't got enough gas to give you to help you out. I'll have to tow you." Patrick hopped off his boat and onto his own. "You'll have to rig up the bridle lines to your d-rings."

The guy may as well have been speaking a foreign language. Patrick clipped the tow lines to the back of his boat and tossed the other ends to Charles. "There are two d-shaped rings at the front of your boat to clip these to. Do you think you can handle that?"

The snide question had Charles fuming.

Of course, he could figure it out. He climbed to the front of the boat, almost slipping off a few times. He'd never been to the front of his boat. He found the rings and clipped the lines to them.

Once Charles was safely back on the deck, Patrick's boat engine rumbled to life.

"Just sit back and relax," Patrick called over his shoulder. "I'll take over for you."

Then Patrick had the gall to wink at him. *I'll take over for you.* Fucking asshole. Charles knew exactly what he meant by that. He'd taken over with Aubrey ... that was a cut that hurt deep.

Patrick.

The guy was a prick—plain and simple.

Chapter Five | Patrick

It had been a low blow and Patrick almost regretted it. Seeing the look on Charles' face as he figured out what he'd meant when he said he'd *take over for him* had been priceless, though.

The guy deserved it.

Patrick picked up a little speed. He needed to keep his speed steady and low while he was towing. No point in wrecking either boat. When he'd got the call that Charles Avery was stranded, he'd almost refused the call, but he'd changed his mind when the image of the arrogant bastard in distress danced through his mind. A grin had spread across his face.

He looked back at his lines. The marina had replaced them recently with a new manufacturer. It was a service the marina offered. Distress calls. He normally didn't work with them, but he'd been asked to take out their new rescue boat to run it through its paces. His expertise when it came to boats was more extensive than his knowledge of the lake. His help was often sought out.

They cruised down the lake for nearly an hour. You could see Kettle Valley and parts of the Lower Mission first, then the city and bridge came into view.

Once in the marina, Patrick flawlessly drifted Charles' boat close enough to the dock that Charles could reach out, grab a line, and tie up the boat. At least Charles knew how to get that right. "Can you unhook those tow lines for me?" Patrick asked Charles.

He smirked as Charles crawled onto the bow of his boat for a second time. What he wouldn't give to have Charles fall into the water. Get his pompous boating clothes soaked.

Once the tow bridle was released, he hauled the equipment onto his deck. He stowed it all away then turned his boat away from the dock. He needed to park it closer to the office.

Charles could figure out his own gas situation. He'd likely have someone at the marina do it. Gas him up and return his boat to its assigned mooring. Charles was one of the more extravagant boat owners with an ostentatious vessel likely stocked full of expensive wine.

A pretentious beast.

Charles.

The guy was a prick—plain and simple.

Chapter Six | Charles

It was a necessity, the wine-tasting event. Quail Run had a booth and there were connections to be made with wine merchants and other wineries. Enticing new consumers to try their wines was simply a bonus. Charles adjusted the collar of his white dress shirt. He'd changed his suit, opting for a casual olive-toned cotton one. He ran his fingers through his hair, working the hair gel. It was the one thing he kept on the wild side of things, his hair. It was spiked to suit his mood tonight.

The whole boat towing incident was infuriating enough, but Patrick showing up at his winery last week, all smiles, his hair up in an absurd bun those hipsters tended to sport, had rankled him even more. The unpleasant interaction was still festering within him. Touching the guy's hand made him feel sick. It was a hand that had caressed Aubrey's skin.

He shivered.

Aubrey had been held in that guy's arms. Kissed by his lips—been made love to by his body. Aubrey had left him for that immature excuse for a man. Not even a man. A young upstart.

He tugged on the cuffs of his shirt.

It had agitated him that the adulteress knew details about his winery. That Aubrey had possibly passed on the knowledge of wines to Patrick. Knowledge that Aubrey had learned from him.

Charles snorted out a laugh.

Patrick the prancing fucking pony. That's all he was. A

vapid party boy that had by chance digested and regurgitated a thing or two about the wine industry and Quail's Run.

Then why had Aubrey left him for the guy? He scanned through their seven-year history. It had to have been something he had done—or hadn't done. It had to have been his fault.

He looked at himself in the mirror. Maybe he was like his father. Incapable of maintaining a healthy relationship. Irreparably flawed.

Undesirable.

He turned and headed down the stairs. His Range Rover was parked in the driveway. At least he had his career. He knew he could do that right. And tonight; was show time. He calmed his nerves with some deep breathing as he climbed into the front seat.

He could do this.

Charles backed out of the driveway. The venue hosting the wine-tasting event was a short drive away. He found a parking spot and headed inside.

The event was fully underway. He headed for the Quail's Run booth. The white tablecloth, the backdrop of their vineyards. Everything looked polished and professional. His best employees were behind the table pouring samples for consumers and industry people and sharing their extensive knowledge. There was a lot of chatter and smiles being exchanged.

It was going well.

He headed further into the room and spotted two people. Aubrey and then Patrick; at opposite ends of the exhibit room. He wasn't sure what direction to head. He opted for the space between them. It was ridiculous; having to maneuver to avoid people.

He was almost at the booth at the back of the room when Aubrey turned and saw him. Of course, Aubrey wasn't alone. Some sexy twink was pressed to his side, touching his arm, and chattering into space. Aubrey wasn't listening. He was focused on Charles. Aubrey lifted the glass he was holding as if offering a toast to Charles.

Charles went numb. He needed to prove to Aubrey that he didn't care anymore. That Aubrey couldn't unnerve him. Laughter to his left had him turning to face it.

Patrick.

Without thinking, Charles headed straight for him. He pushed past a couple of people and placed himself at Patrick's side.

"How's the Chardonnay?" he asked Patrick, startling him.

The closeness: revulsion rolled through Charles. It had been an impulse. Heading Patrick's way. Patrick stepped back, creating some space between them. He scowled at Charles.

"It's buttery. I'm not sure I like it."

Charles pointed to a booth behind Patrick. "Try the Chardonnay from Vista. It's unoaked. It's clean and dry with an enticing aroma of apple."

Patrick narrowed his eyes at Charles then shrugged. It was all the encouragement Charles needed. Patrick let himself be guided to the next booth occupied by Vista Vineyards.

Charles looked over his shoulder. Aubrey was staring intently at them.

Good.

Charles lifted a mini wine glass and held it to his nose. "See ... apple."

Patrick nodded. "Seems more my style." He breathed in the aroma, took a sip, held it in his mouth, and swirled it around a bit. He inhaled a breath. Paused then swallowed.

Charles smiled. Patrick was a swallower—not a spitter. For a moment, he wondered if that extended to Patrick's cock sucking preferences as well.

He shoulder-checked again. Aubrey was still watching them. He looked extremely uncomfortable with him talking to Patrick. He needed to keep it going.

"So ... you grew up in the Okanagan?" Charles asked.

"My whole life."

"Me too."

Patrick discarded his glass and crossed his arms. "What are you doing? Why are you talking to me?" He lifted his gaze and scanned the room. "Oh ... Aubrey."

He stared at Charles. There was a moment of decision in his eyes. "All right, I'm game. I found a Pinot Noir I'd like your opinion on."

"Westend Wineries?"

"No. Tantalizing Vines."

"I heard they'd improved."

"I think you'll be surprised." Patrick led the way. "I tried them a year ago. Didn't like what they had to offer. I decided to give them another chance this year. I'm glad I did."

Charles stared at Patrick as he walked away. He was wearing a pink polo shirt, khaki cargo shorts, and canvas loafers. Charles shook his head. Hardly wine-tasting apparel. And his hair was up in that damned knot, short, fuzzy strands of blond descending onto his neck. Charles hummed to himself. It probably looked much better down; a blond mane cascading atop his shoulders.

And that beard. What was that about? It was sure to leave road rash on a man's skin. On his chin, his cheeks—lips, his inner thighs—his ass. Aubrey had never come home with any of that.

He'd been careful.

Charles cleared his throat and followed Patrick. The guy was genuinely excited by his discovery. It was a welcome distraction after a long day. Exchanging finds with someone enthusiastic about wine had fallen by the wayside in his life. Aubrey had been his wine guy.

He surveyed the room as he crossed it. Aubrey was nowhere to be seen. He could've ended the charade there. Instead, he wandered up beside Patrick. Charles was curious to try the wine Patrick considered a winner. To test the sophistication of his palette.

He held the glass poured for him to his nose. It was hauntingly aromatic. He took a sip and held it. The wine was like velvet on his tongue complimented by smooth, seductive berry flavors. It was gorgeous. Charles swallowed and held up his glass.

Patrick was watching him, anticipation lighting up his brown eyes.

Charles couldn't help but smile. Patrick was like a puppy looking for praise. And he was fully prepared to give it to him. He'd done good. "You have good taste."

"See." Patrick smiled. "I knew you'd like it." Then the curtain of cordiality descended. Patrick looked around. "Aubrey's gone. I think we sufficiently wound him up."

A little rumble of disappointment about Patrick pulling away tickled Charles' gut.

"Serves him right."

Patrick grinned. "I know, right? Did you see that guy he was with? Was he even old enough to be in here? They really shouldn't let children into events like this."

Charles snorted out a chuckle then caught himself. A flush of color rose in his cheeks. It had been forever since someone had made him laugh.

"You're pretty uptight, aren't you?" Patrick stuffed his hands into his pockets.

The guy was direct. He liked that even though it threw him off.

"What do you mean by that?"

Patrick stepped back. "Look at what you're wearing. Your clothes have uptight, pompous ass written all over them."

Charles looked down at his suit. "What's wrong with what I'm wearing? I'm the general manager of an influential winery. What am I supposed to be wearing?"

"Maybe you haven't noticed …" Patrick pointed toward a wall of floor-to-ceiling windows. "It's the middle of a blistering summer. A light cotton suit at the very least."

Charles huffed. "I am not taking fashion advice from you."

Patrick cocked an eyebrow. "It's the bun, isn't it?"

"Yeah, it kind of screams hipster beach bum."

"Fair." Patrick turned and pointed toward a booth. "Want to check out the competitor's Cabernet? Rumor has it, they've cracked the nuances your winery has been screwing up on."

This time Charles fully grinned. Patrick didn't hold back. He spoke his mind.

"You can tell me where we're falling short."

"It would be my pleasure."

They cued up together. "Have you taken any wine-tasting classes?" Charles asked.

Patrick furrowed his brow as he looked at Charles. "No. Should I?"

"I think you have potential. I can suggest some."

"Thanks." Patrick tipped his head. "Why are you being nice to me?"

Charles shook his head. The truth was, he didn't know. Patrick's carefree attitude had sucked him in. Memories of Aubrey leaving him invaded his mind. Cheated on him and left him. Cheated on him with the man standing at his side. He shivered as his skin prickled at the proximity.

He buried his hands in his pockets. "I need to get back to my booth." He rushed away intent on reaching the familiar setting, changed his mind, and headed for the washroom.

He flung the door open and raced for the sink. He was shaking. He turned on the cold water and splashed his face with it. How could he have let this happen? Talking to that asshole. He had only meant to make Aubrey jealous. Not strike up a perverse friendship over wine.

Charles turned off the water and stared at himself in the mirror, replaying Patrick's words. Maybe that was why Aubrey had left him. He straightened his suit jacket and fixed his hair. Was he an obnoxious pompous ass? Uptight. Was Patrick right in his assessment?

It made sense. Aubrey had left him for a carefree, witty guy with a kind face. Someone nothing like him. He stared at his eyes. He wasn't sure there was anyone worthy of love behind them.

"Charles."

One of his employees. "The exhibit is shutting down. Do you want any of these bottles to take home?" He pursed his lips. "And a guy is hanging around waiting for you."

Heat rose into Charles' face. Couldn't the guy take a hint? He was finished with him. Patrick needed to fuck off and leave him alone. It had been a mistake talking to him.

He sped toward the booth, prepared to cause a scene. A man with cropped silver hair wearing a cotton cream-colored suit, looking incredible, approached him.

Charles slowed to a stop.

It was Aubrey. He had a bottle of wine in each hand. He raised them as he walked toward Charles. "Babe … we need to talk."

Charles pushed past him. "I have nothing to say to you."

"Come back to the townhouse. We'll have some wine … go over things."

Charles spun to face him. "Like how you cheated on me. I'm finished talking about that."

Aubrey scowled. "Then, what were you doing talking to Patrick?"

Anger rose in Charles' chest. It was time to strike.

"Maybe I find him compelling. Maybe I'm even interested."

Aubrey coughed out a laugh. "Don't be ridiculous. He's beneath you."

"And he wasn't beneath *you*?"

"He was a toy, babe. He meant nothing."

"You were with him for two years."

"I just needed to get it out of my system. I'm ready now. I still love you."

Charles' legs nearly crumpled. He reached for the table to steady himself. It was his wildest dream that Aubrey still loved him. Still wanted him. He almost ran into Aubrey's arms.

Almost.

He checked his elation with a heavy sigh.

It would only be a matter of time before Aubrey dumped him again. Months at most until Aubrey realized he wasn't worth his time. He couldn't go through that again.

"You need to leave," Charles said.

"But, babe."

"I don't want you to take me back."

Aubrey grabbed Charles' arm. "Because of Patrick? You'll be bored of him in no time. He's naïve and as dense as a concrete wall."

A fury began to burn in Charles' gut.

"I think you're wrong there." The words stuck in his throat, but they needed to be said. Patrick wasn't the vapid prancing pony he had assumed him to be. They hadn't spoken for long, but there was more depth to Patrick than Aubrey was letting on.

A cruel smile spread across Aubrey's face.

"He was better in bed than you. I'll give him that."

There it was. The Aubrey he knew. The vicious son-of-a-bitch that used to torment him. Dangle his insecurities over his head. Make him second guess himself. Gut his confidence.

Charles shook his head. And he'd been ready to let himself be drawn back into that. Willing to box away the bad times so he could hope for the good. And there had been good times. Sometimes for months. Then everything would fall apart, and Aubrey would be in his face blaming him for something that had gone wrong. Tearing him down and refusing to collect the pieces.

"I've asked you to leave."

"Fine. Be an obstinate little bitch." Aubrey slammed the bottles down on the table. "But this is it. I won't give you another chance. No one else will put up with your bullshit."

Charles' core was shaking but he was determined to hold fast.

"Then I guess I'll be alone."

Over Aubrey's shoulder, Charles caught movement. Not one of his employees. They were all tearing down the booth beside him. Not the disbursing crowds. It was someone who was deliberately walking toward them, staring, his mouth slack, tears streaming down his cheeks.

Patrick.

He'd heard the whole thing.

Aubrey spun around to face Patrick. He had seen Charles staring over his shoulder. "And there he is. Your new boyfriend." He burst past Patrick, slammed against his shoulder, and knocked him out of the way. "Be sure to fuck him hard. He likes that."

Charles furrowed his brow. "I'm sorry. You shouldn't have heard that."

"I'm glad I did." Patrick rattled some keys in his pocket with one hand. Wiped away a few streaks of tears with the other. "Are you allowed to pull a bottle from your booth's stock?"

"Absolutely … why?"

"Grab a bottle or two. I suspect we have some things to talk about."

Chapter Seven | Patrick

The warm wind reminded Patrick why he loved living in the Okanagan. Summers were glorious for those who worshipped the sun and were captives of the water. Beaches and watersports filled most days for him. When summer retreated, so did he. Relegated to the bar scene.

But that was the last thing on his mind tonight.

The tink-tink-tink of the sailboat masts filled the air. The walkway was lit all the way down to the yacht club. His boss had a boat there that he was able to access. He had the spare keys. It was closer than heading to Charles' boat docked on the other side of town.

They walked in silence, taking alternating swigs of wine straight from a bottle.

Patrick's world had been ripped apart tonight. He'd spent two years with a guy he had thought loved him. At a minimum, had some affection for him. To find out he hadn't—he was gutted.

He unlocked the metal, mesh door to the club's pier. He headed down the ramp. Charles plodded along behind him. When Patrick reached his boss's boat, he stepped down into it.

"Come on." Patrick grabbed the second bottle of wine from Charles' grasp so Charles could steady himself as he boarded the boat.

Patrick dropped down on the white leather bench seating

at the back of the boat. Charles slid in beside him. Patrick opened the second bottle and took a long gulp of the Merlot. Tonight, wasn't for taste testing. Tonight, the wine was being used to get good and drunk.

They stared up at the stars for a long time. The slosh of the wine entering the bottles' necks was the only thing accompanying the sound of the boats tinking and groaning.

Charles was the first to speak.

"When did you meet him?"

"June. He came on one of my boat tours with clients."

"When did you start seeing him?"

"About a month later."

"He broke up with me in the fall." Charles turned to face Patrick. "Did you know about me?"

"That you were still together—no, I had no idea."

Charles grunted.

"You thought I knew," Patrick said.

"How could you not know? I have no idea how he managed to split his time. I knew he was up to something. You had to have suspected."

Charles licked his lips.

It distracted Patrick for a moment.

"I thought he was busy with his job. Clients were always phoning and texting. He used to run off in the middle of our dates. I didn't think anything of it."

"Well … now we know what he was really doing."

"You must hate me."

"You have no idea." Charles took another swig of wine.

"I really didn't know. I never would have started dating him if I knew he was still with you."

"You must have thought he was quite the catch."

Patrick held the bottle to his lips, then lowered it. "What's that supposed to mean?"

"Didn't you ever wonder why he was with you?"

"All the time ... what's your point?"

Charles shook his head. "Nothing. I'm being a prick."

"No, I want to know what you were going to say."

"Okay." Charles looked at him. "I always figured you were a vapid blond boy toy."

Patrick snorted out a laugh.

Charles smiled. "Patrick the prancing fucking pony."

Patrick shrieked with laughter. "You called me that."

"It wasn't my finest moment." Charles took a slug of wine.

"And are you ...? Patrick rested the bottle on his knee. "Aubrey told me you were a callous, controlling, abusive monster that tormented him."

"Pfft." Charles rolled his eyes.

"So, I'm guessing you're not actually a tyrant," Patrick added.

Charles snorted. "The furthest thing from it. I'm a pushover."

Patrick wasn't sure he believed Charles. The things Aubrey had told him. They were detailed and graphic. If Charles was telling the truth, there could only be one explanation.

"The stories Aubrey told me about you ... they were really about him, weren't they?"

"That would be my guess." Charles tapped Patrick's arm. "How was he with you? Did he treat you like a shiny object to be controlled and gaslit?"

"He tried a couple of times. Attempted to twist my

words. Break my confidence. It didn't end well for him. He kept pushing, though. I'm embarrassed to say he was wearing me down."

"Were you in love with him?"

"Yeah, but I could see where he was pulling me."

"And you were prepared to let him."

Patrick nodded. "Shit." He dragged his hand across his hair. He ended at the knot. "We're a fine pair."

Charles held his bottle out until Patrick tapped his to it.

"To a couple of suckers." Charles laughed. "Seven years. Seven fucking years."

"I only managed to entertain him for two."

"That doesn't make me feel any better."

"Wasn't meant to." Patrick shoved Charles with his shoulder, grinning. He looked over at the man by his side. Charles' nice suit was rumpled now. The buttons on his once crisp shirt open to the waist. He could see the pendant on the chain around Charles' neck was a Celtic wolf.

"What's that mean?" Patrick pressed his finger to the silver disk.

"Depends. It can mean chaos and destruction."

"Fuck, that's not good."

"It can also mean bravery, loyalty, protection, and wisdom."

"Ha. You can eliminate most of those."

Charles leaned away from Patrick. "Do you just say whatever pops into your head?"

"Usually. Gets me in a lot of trouble."

"No doubt … I think you're right, though." Charles sighed. "I've been an idiot. I have no idea what he saw in me in the first place. Talk about being a boy toy."

Now Patrick really shoved Charles' shoulder. "Are you kidding me? You have your life together. Smart—talented. A fancy career." He poked Charles' chest. "I bet you're set up real estate wise too. You're the prime example of an eligible bachelor."

"And how would you know what makes anyone eligible? You're like some kind of a drifter."

"I resent that."

"Good. You were meant to."

Patrick furrowed his brow. "Do you still hate me?"

"It's become a habit." Charles leaned back and looked up at the sky.

In the last few minutes, they had both started slurring. Things were getting sloppy. Patrick was having a good time. The banter was unexpected and the company tolerable.

Patrick took a good look at Charles. Even in the dim light, Patrick could see that Charles' face was flushed from the wine. There was a glow of crimson on his tanned skin. He could imagine another way to see that face flushed. In contrast to white sheets, glistening with perspiration.

Charles flung off his posh sandals. Even his toes were beautiful.

The guy was just straight up and down elegant.

"Fucking hell, you're beautiful."

Patrick slammed his hand over his mouth. He hadn't meant to say that aloud.

Charles scrambled to his feet. "I have to go."

"I'm sorry. It just slipped out." He grabbed Charles's arm. "It was just an observation."

Charles scowled at him, then sat back down. "Don't do that again."

"Promise." Patrick made the sign of the cross on his chest. He looked at the two empty wine bottles. It was a sad sight. Might as well keep the party going. He stumbled to his feet. His boss had some scotch in the cabin. He could replace it with most of his next paycheck.

"Where are you going?" Charles grabbed the back of Patrick's shirt.

"More booze." Patrick fumbled with the keys, then popped open the cabin door. He nearly fell down the steep stairs. He rooted through the cupboards, found the liquid that would completely obliterate them, and returned to the boat's deck.

He offered the bottle to Charles.

"This feels like a bad idea." Charles took a swallow, then lowered the bottle, laughing and coughing. "A really bad idea."

"Yeah … whatever." Patrick sat back beside Charles and took the bottle from him. The liquid slipped down his throat, burning warmth into his toes.

Charles heaved out a sigh. "I have to pee." He rose to his feet and headed for the cabin.

"Are you kidding me?" Patrick leaped up. He grabbed Charles' arm. "Don't use the cabin washroom. You'll be filling up the holding tank."

The shocked look on Charles' face as Patrick dragged him to the back of the boat had Patrick wondering if Charles had ever really lived. Free and unencumbered. Not a worry in the world.

Patrick stood on the ledge above the bench seating, fighting to keep his balance. He undid his fly and released the pressure that had been building. Charles was reluctant but he joined him.

Patrick smiled. He liked the idea that he was corrupting Charles in some small way. He climbed down. "Want to go swimming?"

Charles screwed up his face. "What? Now?"

"It's a warm night." Patrick grabbed the bottle and stepped up and out of the boat onto the dock. As he walked, he looked back at Charles as he fell in step behind him.

The overhead light from the pier fell on Charles. His dark hair was messed up like he'd just tumbled out of bed, his chest exposed, pants rumpled, and feet bare. He had his suit jacket thrown over one shoulder. His sandals hung off the fingers of his other hand.

Charles looked like he was walking a high-end fashion runway.

The guy was fucking gorgeous.

Patrick scrubbed a hand across his face to clear the lurid thoughts from his mind, then led him through the security gate, a distance along the walkway, and onto a wide, deserted beach. He had expected there would be more people out on a stifling night like this. Instead, they were alone.

Probably for the best. Neither of them had a swimsuit.

He was the first to strip down to his underwear. Charles held back. Patrick figured he just needed a little bit of liquid courage, so he handed Charles the scotch bottle. Charles took another couple of swigs, stuck the bottle in the sand, and started to remove his clothes.

Patrick wandered down to the water's edge. He turned, ankle-deep in the water. He couldn't take his eyes off Charles. There was enough light from the pavilion bordering the beach that he could see the contours of Charles' body. Toned and tanned, Charles looked goddamned delicious.

He stopped staring when Charles looked up and caught him.

Patrick hummed to himself. Charles was wearing a dusty rose thong. Perhaps he had a wilder side after all. Patrick turned toward the water and dashed into it. It was cold and refreshing after a long hot day. He ducked beneath the gentle, rippling waves. When he emerged, he undid the band holding his hair, tipped his head back, and let the water fan his hair out. The long, thick, blond strands stuck to his back and shoulders when he lifted his head.

Charles was timid as he entered the water. Gasping and sucking in breaths as he waded deeper. After a few starts and stops, he was in the water up to his chest. Patrick swam toward Charles to keep him from walking out further. He was conscious of keeping them from drifting too far away from the shore in the gentle current. They were drunk. Swimming wasn't really a good idea.

Patrick splashed a wash of water into Charles' face. He got a grin in return, then Charles disappeared beneath the surface. He came up, his spikey hair now laying flat against his head. The light from the beach pavilion danced across the water, illuminating them both.

Charles smiled and blinked, and Patrick's heart nearly stopped. Charles' lashes were long and wet, forming exquisite inky peaks. An image of Charles towering over him, gazing into his soul with those eyes invaded his mind. Charles' full, rosy lips poised to kiss him.

"You need to stop staring at me."

Patrick cleared his throat. "I'm sorry. I'm drunk."

Charles swam a few feet from him, then treaded water to keep himself upright even though they were shallow enough to keep their feet on the ground.

Patrick gravitated toward him. He could see it made Charles uncomfortable; the close proximity, but he couldn't stop himself. He had the urge to hang off Charles in that water like a damned monkey. Wrap his legs around his waist, his arms around his neck—and attack his mouth.

"I really should go. Call a taxi and head home." Charles walked toward the shore and emerged. Patrick caught a glorious look at his ass as Charles made his way up the beach to his clothes; the material of the thong buried deep between two round, sculpted, powerful muscles.

Patrick's breathing grew ragged. This was insane. He needed to stop looking. He sunk below the water as Charles left the beach and headed for the walkway and the nearest roadway.

Fuck.

He hadn't been that drawn to someone in a very long time.

Chapter Eight | Charles

Charles leaned forward on his desk and put his forehead on the stack of papers littering the desktop. He was suffering. Headache—nausea. He hadn't drunk that much in ages. Patrick had been a bad influence. His party-boy persona had come out in full force last night.

He sighed. It had been surprisingly cathartic. After a devastating blow-up with Aubrey, hanging with Patrick had been exactly what he needed.

He still hated the guy.

He couldn't believe Patrick was unaware that Aubrey was two-timing him.

How could he not know? Aubrey always came home to him every night. Patrick should have suspected something when Aubrey refused to stay overnight. And why Aubrey never invited Patrick back to his place ... Charles lifted his head. Maybe Aubrey had. Maybe they had met at their home during the day while he was at work. Made love in their bed. Soiled their sheets.

Charles shivered.

He had come home to fresh sheets often that summer. He thought Aubrey had become fastidious about laundry. And then Aubrey had made love to him in them.

Made love?

It hadn't been love. It had been possession. Aubrey had just been fucking him.

Charles woke up his computer screen with his mouse. He had some production spreadsheets to review. After that a presentation for staff, thanking them for their hard work.

Then he'd stretch out on the sofa in his office and have a nap.

He closed his eyes. Patrick had let his hair out of that ridiculous bun while they were in the water. It had tumbled onto his shoulders; wet, seductive ropes of dark blond.

He grunted.

The scene had caught his cock's attention. He'd only just managed to make it below the waterline before Patrick noticed the state of it. Patrick had been staring again.

A knock on his door. "Charles?" The production manager, Carlos. "Could you have those spreadsheets back to me soon? I need to make some adjustments before I place any orders."

"Have you heard from Duncan yet? Are we ready to start harvest next week?"

"That's the plan."

"I better get this done then." Charles moved his mouse again and the screen came to life. It would take him less than an hour to go through everything.

He was busy, but the rest of the day crawled by. He managed a twenty-minute nap, but that only made him want to crawl back into bed. He barely made it to the end of the day.

As he pulled into his driveway, he was ready to drag himself inside and crash. The front door didn't open soon enough. The stairs; a mountainous terrain. He fell on his bed fully clothed.

Charles had one day a week off and it was tomorrow. He

was going to enjoy it. Lounge around in his air-conditioned house. Maybe take his boat out. Have an extravagant meal.

He shut his eyes. The last thing on his mind was a tender, bloody steak.

And Patrick's damned hair.

It was pitch black when he awoke hours later. He padded down the stairs into the kitchen. He was hungry, but the fridge didn't look too promising.

He had two options. Order delivery or brave the crowds and go out for a late dinner. He groaned. He was sick of the delivery option. Burgers, sushi, or pizza didn't sound appealing. He would keep it simple. Head for the local gay lounge and order a few appetizers to fill himself up.

He changed into some casual apparel. Tailored but laid-back. The drive there was quiet. No music. He needed the silence to prepare himself for the noise and chaos he was about to walk into. A quiet meal at a steak house was more in line with what he was looking for. But the pull to be around his own people was strong tonight. Aubrey's words would be stinging for a while.

As expected, the place was crowded. It was a Saturday night. Queers and drag queens filled the place. Charles caught the owner, Mario's eye, and waved to him. Mario was set up at a table in the middle of the lounge's patio. He called Charles over. There was one seat left. There were definite benefits to knowing the owner. Mario bought his Merlot and Cabernet from Quail's Run. They had struck up a friendship of sorts. A friendship over the appreciation of the finer things.

He walked toward the table.

Dammit.

Charles recognized the knotted hair in the seat next to the empty one.

Patrick.

"We meet again," Charles said to Patrick as he pulled out his chair and sat down.

"Oh, hey." Patrick lifted a wine glass to his lips.

Charles' eyebrows rose. "How on earth can you be drinking already?"

"Youth."

Charles grinned. "Fuck off. I'm not that much older than you."

"I'm going to guess eight years."

"That would make me twenty-seven."

"Ha—ha."

Mario cleared his throat from across the table. "Charles. How's the wine business?"

"Flourishing."

"Perfect. Good to hear. They've got a good man at the helm."

"I appreciate the confidence."

"Young Patrick here knows a bit about wine." Mario slammed his hand on the table. A few people jumped. "But, of course, you already know each other."

Charles scowled. Had Patrick been telling the entire table about their drunk escapades last night? He was just about to push his chair out and make his way to a steak restaurant.

"Our silver fox, Aubrey," Mario added. "Perhaps you two should adjust your seating. I'd hate to see a fight break out."

Patrick raised his glass. "No, we're fine."

The table went back to their conversations.

"So," Patrick said to Charles. "I'm twenty-nine."

Charles' eyebrows rose. "You're older than I thought."

"I credit my sunscreen."

"I'm not a user."

"And it suits you."

Charles grunted. Another *observation*, as Patrick had called it, that wasn't welcome.

"Thirty-five," he said. "You're wrong by two years."

"It's the sun. It ages you."

"Are you saying I have wrinkles?"

"A few around your eyes when you smile."

"Then I need to stop smiling."

Patrick tipped his head to one side. "Please don't do that."

Charles sighed. Patrick was doing it again. The compliments—the staring. He was probably wondering what beyond his looks Aubrey had seen in him. Aside from his physical allure and money, he had very little to offer. He'd never had any luck socializing with the group around him. They simply tolerated him because Mario had taken a shine to him.

He was the shy, quiet guy in the corner.

"I can stop smiling if I want to," Charles said. "Why do you care?"

Patrick crossed his arms. "I don't."

"Fine. Good." Charles turned his back to Patrick and leaned into the conversation on his left. He wasn't good at jumping in, but he was going to make an effort, so he didn't have to speak to Patrick anymore. His neighbors were talking politics. Discussing the anti-SOGI protestors.

Patrick shoved his chair out next to him. Charles turned so he could see him. Patrick was headed for the bar. He was wearing a ratty blue t-shirt, swim trunks, and flip-flops. Not a care in the world. Charles anticipated Patrick would be returning to the table, but Patrick wasn't getting another drink. He was settling his bill. Charles had successfully run him off.

It almost didn't sit right with him.

Ultimately, he didn't care if he'd hurt Patrick's feelings. One night of drunkenness didn't equal a warped friendship. The guy had slept in his bed—with his partner. He was sure of it. Surely, Patrick would have looked around? Seen the photos of him and Aubrey. Noticed there was stuff on both bedside tables. Patrick was lying to him. He'd known he wasn't the only one.

Charles leaned back in his chair. His heart was aching again. He'd been replaced. The only man he had ever loved had replaced him with a hot, younger version. He should have seen it coming. Aubrey was pushing sixty. Confident and gorgeous. Both he and Patrick had found Aubrey's mature charm captivating. They had that in common, but Patrick was the enemy.

Someone grabbed his shoulder.

"I *do* care," Patrick said from behind him. "I care because your eyes light up when you smile. And I think you need more of that in your life."

Oh, for fuck's sake.

Charles chose to ignore him. Eventually, Patrick left him alone. Left the lounge. But it stuck with him—Patrick's words. *You need more of that in your life.*

Exactly what was he implying? That he was devoid of

joy? He had plenty of it. The winery brought him immense satisfaction. Why had Patrick come back to tell him that?

Just to be bloody annoying. He was sure of it.

His appetizers came but he only ate half of them. Patrick had upset his gut. What the hell was Patrick doing looking at his eyes in the first place? He felt violated.

He offered his apologies for leaving early, left a wad of cash on the table, and headed back to his car. He didn't want to go home yet, so he headed for a beach along the way.

Once parked, he took off his shoes and wandered out onto the sand. It was a clear, warm night. There wouldn't be too many more of those. Third week of August, those tended to disappear. The weather turned cool at night. Then a pleasant September. Then October … all frigid hell could break loose. A few months after that and they'd be harvesting the grapes for ice wine.

He slipped his hands into his pockets and just wandered, digging his toes into the sand. Charles relished the link to nature that came with winemaking. It felt organic and fundamentally linked to history. Humans had been producing wine for a very long time.

It sang to his soul.

Charles bent over and rolled up his pant legs. He walked into the waves up to his calves. The coolness swirled around his skin. Annoyingly, it reminded him of last night and his drunken swim with Patrick. Of seeing Patrick stripped down to his underwear. He'd watched him undress. Patrick had the body of a runner. Lean and muscular.

He took a stroll down to the far end of the beach and back again. Patrick's words were playing in his mind. Not just from tonight at the lounge. But from last night as well.

The things Patrick had said to him and the ease by which the cutting banter had flowed between them weren't sitting well with him. He stared down at his feet. He hadn't known Aubrey had made him out to be such a monster. Filled Patrick's head with reasons to hate him.

They'd cleared that up. Or had they? It was just his word against Aubrey's. Charles could be lying as readily about being an abuser as Patrick was about his cheating.

Maybe he and Aubrey had been equally toxic. Maybe they had abused each other. Patrick had no way of knowing the truth.

Charles furrowed his brow.

Patrick didn't need to know the truth. It made no difference to anything. He looked out across the lake. Patrick was definitely lying about the affair. He was sure of it.

He hated the guy.

He kicked the water. Then why was he so drawn to him? His scrubby beard, and curly tendrils of blond hair on his neck. His soft brown eyes filled with kindness.

Even the way he moved. Confident but casual. Striding along in his tacky shoes.

The whole package was calling to him.

Fuck.

Charles stormed toward his car. He needed more sleep. Sleep and a stiff drink when his body would allow him to have one. He threw the car into drive and pulled out onto the street.

He didn't even see the other vehicle; he was so distracted. The speeding pickup truck hit his driver's side door with a sickening screech and crunch. The airbag exploded in his face. His head hit the headrest. Tumbling—spinning. Time felt suspended as his body was carried by the force. Two rotations and his car skidded, landed on its roof, and rocked in place.

He didn't remember anything after that.

The room was dimly lit as he opened his eyes, then the full force of the pain his body had been enduring rocketed through every fiber of his being.

Charles groaned and reached for anything to help him sit up.

"Whoa, whoa … take it easy. You don't need to get up."
You've got to be fucking kidding me.

What the hell was Patrick doing there? And where was he? He wasn't at home in bed. Patrick hadn't broken into his house. He groaned. A vague relocation seeped into his mind. He remembered the shock of the impact. The feeling of spinning. The sharp pain in his neck as his head was thrown around. Then the screaming pain in his shoulder and across his hips as the seatbelt cut into him.

His thigh—God, his thigh.

It had all gone black after that. Now that he'd recalled the details of the accident, the panic and pain seared themselves into his mind. All of that was nothing compared to the agony he was in now. He needed pain meds.

"Do you want me to call someone?" Patrick touched Charles' hand. The sensation of Patrick's hand irritated Charles. A mixture of revulsion plus a calming tingle. He scanned the room.

It had to be a hospital.

Charles nodded which sent sparks of agony up and down

his spine. Even his eye sockets hurt. His cheeks, his chin—his jaw. He reached up with one hand. His face was swollen. There were butterfly bandages along one eyebrow. And his lips were split and dry.

He surveyed the rest of his injuries. His arm was in a cast. One of his legs was in traction and screaming for drugs. And the pain in his ribs made it hard to take in a proper breath. He thanked whatever gods had been looking out for him. It could have been so much worse.

"I'll be right back." Patrick patted Charles' shoulder and took off out through the door.

Seriously. What is he doing here?

When Patrick returned, he had a nurse with him and a plastic cup of ice water. Charles was so thirsty; he didn't care who was holding the straw to his lips. Patrick stood there patiently as he almost drained the entire cup. He even managed a mumble of thanks.

"Your boyfriend says you're in pain," the nurse said.

"I am. Not my boyfriend."

"Only family is allowed in here today." The nurse checked the medication pump to the left of Charles' bed. She keyed in a few things on the machine, then squeezed his IV solution bag.

Charles sighed. The truth was, he didn't want to be alone. He was in agony and felt vulnerable. "He is … he is my boyfriend." His hatred of Patrick would have to take a backseat.

The nurse left the room.

"I'll stay a bit longer. But that doesn't mean we're friends," Patrick said.

"That goes without saying." Charles fiddled with his

gown. "Why *are* you here?"

"Couldn't sleep. I was headed to the beach. Saw the accident."

"That doesn't answer my question."

"I saw them pull you out of your car." Patrick looked at his hands. "Just about had a heart attack when I recognized you. I followed the ambulance here."

Charles narrowed his eyes at Patrick. "But why?"

"Honestly. You seem a little lost and alone in the world. Thought you could use someone here when you woke up."

Charles rolled his eyes. "I have plenty of people."

Patrick crossed his arms. "Yeah? Who? Who would you like me to call?"

There was a long pause as they glared at each other.

Charles released an exasperated breath. "All right. I don't have anyone. Satisfied?"

"Really? There's no one?" Patrick untangled his arms and gripped the bedrail. "I didn't want to be right. I was just trying to rile you up."

Charles looked away. Patrick was staring at him with pity. "My dad died three years ago, and I don't have any siblings."

"What about friends?"

"None in town, except casual ones. But this would be a bit heavy for them."

"Nice friends you have."

"Don't start with me."

Patrick put his hands up. "Okay. Okay. I'll leave it alone."

Charles turned back to look at Patrick. "You don't have to stay."

"If I go, who is going to bring you ice water?"

"I'm sure the nurses' aides will keep me topped up."

Patrick smiled. "Then who is going to harass you about what a mess your face is? That airbag did a number on you."

Charles grunted and closed his eyes. His mind was getting fuzzy. They could continue this later. Right now, he needed sleep. The drugs were kicking in and he was starting to drift away.

"Thanks for coming," he mumbled. It was the truth. He was thankful to have someone there. Even if it was Patrick. He found the guy alternately aggravating and soothing. Like a tug-o-war happening in his head. In his drugged state, he might have voiced it aloud, the conflict.

Instead, he fell asleep.

When he awoke, the chair at his bedside was empty.

The void, the absence of the man he should be hating caused a crushing ache in his chest. He had to remind himself that Patrick had been fucking Aubrey right under his nose.

There was no room for forgiveness.

He stared at the door.

Then why was he hoping Patrick would come walking back through it?

Chapter Nine | Patrick

Patrick's head dipped as he nodded off, jerking and startling him. He looked toward the bed. Charles was sleeping again. They'd upped his medication because they were taking him down for a scan soon and wanted him to be comfortable for it. The increase had knocked him out.

An hour ago, Charles had awoken crying out. Begging for help with the pain. It had distressed Patrick to no end to see him vulnerable like that. His views regarding Charles were evolving. He'd done a lot of soul-searching while he sat there, going over every bit of the conversation he and Charles had shared while on that boat. He had decided to believe Charles. That Aubrey had been the abuser in his relationship with Charles. That Charles was as gentle and meek as he proclaimed.

It tracked.

Aubrey, once Patrick moved in with him, had started to exhibit some control tendencies. He always wanted to know where Patrick was going, who he would be with—when he was coming home. And if he didn't come home exactly when he said he would, Aubrey would blow up his phone with texts and calls. Then he'd get a guilt trip about worrying Aubrey when he arrived home.

The guy in the hospital bed wouldn't have been as strong as him in resisting Aubrey. In the few conversations they'd had, Charles seemed very unsure of himself. Like he'd been beaten down at some point in his life. Maybe more than once. It seemed ingrained.

Patrick rubbed his lips. He knew Charles still hated him, but he wasn't going to leave him alone in that bed. No one should be alone, regardless of their differences. Especially this man. He was so incredibly drawn to him. A constant flutter of warm feelings unnerved him.

Charles had fallen short of telling him to leave. He'd suggested that Patrick didn't need to be there a few times. But he hadn't ordered him out.

Now that Charles was settled, Patrick took the opportunity to rest his eyes. He'd had to leave to do a shift on the boat, but he'd headed right back to the hospital afterward. He hadn't had a proper sleep in three days. Just a few hours here and there in the chair.

"You still here?"

Patrick rose to his feet and approached the bed. "Yup. Had to go to work for a bit but I'm back for a few hours. I need to go home for a shower and a proper sleep."

"God … a shower. That would be amazing."

"None of those in your near future." Patrick tapped Charles' leg which was in traction. "How long does the doc say you'll be in this contraption?"

"At least eight weeks. Maybe more."

"Who's running the winery."

"The owner is bringing in someone from another branch. Ontario, I think. She's green. But she's eager. I'll be zooming with her every day to keep her on track."

"How's your pain?"

"Manageable."

Patrick leaned on the bed rail. "I enrolled in one of those

wine courses you recommended."

Charles smiled. "You're going to love it."

"Not sure why I'm doing it. It's not going to improve by boat tour skills."

"For the enjoyment of it."

"Easy for you to say. The fees are a pittance for you. For me, it's a lot of money to put out for a hobby. I had to take some dreaded bartending shifts to cover it."

Charles studied Patrick's face. "What if I made you a deal?'

Patrick placed his chin on his arms resting on the bed rail. "I like deals."

"Finish the entire series of courses and I'll give you a job at the winery."

Say what?

The drugs must be doing a serious number on Charles.

"You're stoned."

"Maybe, but you have potential. I like to curate the best staff in the valley."

"And you think that's me."

"Could be."

He wouldn't have to think about it for long. The opportunity to work at a winery was a dream job. An actual career. "Full-time?"

"If that's what you want."

There had to be a catch. Charles was drawing him in until he let his guard down, then he'd pounce. It was a trap. Charles still hated him. The conversations they'd had in that hospital room for days had been superficial. It made no sense why he was even there staying with Charles.

"Why are you doing this?" Patrick asked.

"I told you. I like to have the best staff."

"But you still believe I knew about you and Aubrey."

Charles clenched his jaw. "I've been considering the possibility that you didn't know. Unless you've only been staying here with me because you feel guilty."

"I don't do guilt."

"Of course, you don't."

"What's that supposed to mean?" Patrick straightened up and threw his hands into the air. "What do I have to do to convince you I didn't know you were still with Aubrey? Seriously, Charles. What? Tell me. I'll do it. I hate this fucking rift between us."

"Why do you care about any damned rift?"

Patrick ran his hands across the top of his head and knitted his fingers together, resting them there. "Because maybe I'm starting to like you a little bit."

Charles sat up. "Get out."

He didn't need to be told twice. It had been a stupid thing to say. Patrick left the room and raced down the hall to the elevator. The words had been playing on his tongue for days. Charles had been haunting his dreams. The accident. The feeling of absolute panic he had felt.

He pressed the elevator button.

As he passed the coffee shop, he remembered how he had intended to grab a latte on the way out, expecting that he'd be leaving feeling elated by being in Charles' presence. Now, he couldn't stand to be in the hospital a moment longer. He drove to the marina and took out a boat.

Out on the water, he could breathe again. He traveled down the lake. To one side were the vineyards of the Quail's Run winery. Atop the hill, the building Charles worked in every day.

He turned the boat away. He felt like he was stalking the guy. He hadn't meant to drive to that part of the lake. He'd been drawn there. Charles was under his skin.

Patrick geared up the speed on the boat, cresting and crashing over the waves. He'd screwed that up, telling Charles what he was feeling. His gut twisted. It was almost perverse, longing for his ex's ex. He needed to bury his attraction. Distract himself.

He slowed the boat, pulled out his phone, and opened a gay dating app. There were a few guys to choose from. All within walking distance of the marina. He brought the boat back to the dock, secured it, and tossed the keys into the office. He sent the closest guy a message.

An address popped up on his screen. The guy wasn't looking for anything other than a good fuck. He entered the hotel at the address and headed for room 310. As he stood there looking at the guy, he couldn't help but feel like he'd be cheating on Charles.

Fuck.

He couldn't do it.

He made his apologies and took off. Walking down the street, he felt like screaming. His mind was so full of a man he couldn't have, his head was buzzing with anguish. It had snuck on him. At first, he'd only been attracted to Charles' looks. Then they'd shared stories of heartache because of Aubrey while on that boat, and the conversations they'd had in the hospital room—getting to know each other. Something had shifted in Patrick. Charles had become a real person. Not just someone he could hate for reasons he didn't even know were the truth.

And he kind of liked that real person. He liked the way Charles had been so timid about relieving himself off the back of the boat. How he'd thrown off caution and joined him to swim in the lake. His shy looks and smiles. The jabs and banter. The man behind the fancy suits and money.

Patrick walked into the gay lounge and found a seat. It was quiet mid-week. He ordered a tumbler of expensive scotch. Four more after that and he was starting to feel better. He'd have to work double shifts next week to cover the cost of extravagance. He didn't care.

He slammed the last empty glass on the table. If he started now, it would take him twenty minutes to walk to the hospital. He had a few things on his mind he wanted Charles to hear.

He stepped outside. It was scorching hot out. He'd need water at the very least. It suddenly became too complicated. He thought better of walking and called a cab.

Patrick walked through the doors of the hospital. He straightened up as he strode past the nurses' station, not wanting them to know he was drunk. He stumbled into Charles' room.

"I thought I got rid of you," Charles said.

"I have some things to say to you." Patrick gripped Charles' bed rail.

"You're drunk."

Patrick held up one finger. "Correct."

"I have no interest in you telling me anything."

"Too bad. You're a captive audience." He leaned heavily against the bed. His legs were deceiving him. "You have to listen to me. You have no choice."

Patrick stared at Charles. The swelling in his face was

decreasing. His beauty was re-emerging. Charles would have a few scars, but they'd fade over time.

Charles did his best to cross his arms with his cast on.

"Then I guess I'm going to be subjected to your nonsense."

"It's not nonsense." Patrick grabbed Charles' shoulder. "I have a confession."

"I think you've already done that."

"It's more than that." Patrick shook his finger in front of Charles' face. "I almost slept with a guy this afternoon. But I couldn't do it … because of you."

Charles' chest heaved. "You've lost your mind."

"Maybe. But I can't stop thinking about you."

"Okay, enough." Charles shook his head. "You've said your piece. Now get out of here."

Patrick put his hand on Charles' arm. "I need you to know something. It's our conversations that have put me in this headspace. Sure, you're beautiful, but you're so much more than that."

"You really are insane."

"You don't believe that, do you? That you're more than your looks." Patrick stepped back. "I don't understand that. Did Aubrey do that to you?"

"You tell me. You fucked him in my bed."

"Oh, for fuck's sake. I never slept with him in your bed."

"My sheets were too damned clean all summer."

Patrick huffed breath after breath out through his nose. "What do I have to do to convince you? Suck you off right here in this hospital room? I'll do it." He approached the bed. He would too. He'd fucking whip those covers off and give Charles the best blow job he'd ever had.

Then he remembered he was drunk.

He stumbled. Best not to make statements like that.

Charles rolled the covers down and lifted his gown. "Go for it."

Patrick nearly fell forward. Charles' soft cock lay atop full, delicate pink balls. It was bloody tempting. He almost reached out and touched it.

Drunk, drunk, drunk.

"Come on," Charles said. "Suck and swallow. I dare you."

"Rain check." Patrick stepped back. He dashed from the room and almost ran into a staff member. What the hell had he been thinking? Opening up to Charles and offering to suck him off.

Charles was right. He was right off his rocker.

Chapter Ten | Charles

Charles pulled his gown back down and drew the blankets up to cover his chest. For a second, he had thought Patrick was gearing up to go through with it; suck his cock.

He would've stopped him. He had no desire to have Patrick's mouth around his cock. He leaned back against the pillow and closed his eyes.

Liar.

The possibility was a recurring dream that plagued him. Patrick's wide, warm tongue—his lips around his length. The rough abrasion of his mustache and beard on his skin.

His cock responded to the image.

He placed his hand on it through the blankets to discourage it.

The guy fascinated him, that's all. He was curious to know what Aubrey had seen in Patrick. That's why he had offered Patrick a job at the winery.

Again. Liar.

He detested Patrick, but he was drawn to him. It was infuriating and confusing. Especially because Patrick had expressed an attraction to him for reasons beyond his looks. Patrick had said he'd seen something more. He wanted to believe him.

No one else will put up with your bullshit.

Aubrey's words.

Charles groaned. Patrick was delusional.

Fuck.

Those lips of his. Pink peeking out from between course, dark blond hair. The guy was kissable. Kissable and fuckable. Charles put his hand over his eyes. He would never degrade Patrick by reducing him to that. A fuckable object. He was sweet and kind and had been there for him when no one else had. He'd spent days in that damned chair. That took some dedication.

But was it guilt that kept him in that chair?

Was it guilt that made Patrick say those things?

So many things had been said that shouldn't have been said in his life.

The scene with his father washed in. Feeble and bewildered, his dad hadn't even tried to fight for his mom's love. He'd immersed himself in his winery. He'd tried his best with Charles, but Charles had a habit of screwing up. He was never able to live up to his dad's expectations. When he'd come out to his dad and told him he was gay, his father had disowned him. All the years of his dad calling him a pretty sissy boy culminated in being abandoned.

He was a fuck up.

After that, every relationship he'd ever had reaffirmed that. Picked up like a pretty penny then discarded when it was discovered he had no real worth.

Aubrey had been his longest relationship. They'd even talked about getting married. Maybe children. Charles heaved out a sigh. He was so glad they hadn't dragged kids into their mess.

He wanted a family, but it had to be with the right person.

If he was even out there.

Charles stared up at the ceiling. At least at work, he excelled. Years of trying to get things right with his dad had made him a perfectionist. Even still, he always fell short of his goals.

Patrick's words echoed in his ears.

Sure, you're beautiful, but you're so much more than that.

A small sliver of hope seeped in. Maybe Patrick hadn't been lying about knowingly sleeping with Audrey while they were still together. And maybe Patrick had even been telling the truth about the attraction he had expressed—and why. That his feelings went beyond skin deep.

Charles lifted his phone. He didn't even have Patrick's phone number. He felt like he needed to apologize. Patrick had put his life on hold for days to sit in his hospital room.

Patrick didn't deserve to be run off.

The sun set that night and Patrick didn't return.

Every day for the next nine weeks, Charles stared at his door every time there was movement in the hallway. It was never Patrick. The days dragged on without his company. The dreams persisted. Patrick's mouth on his. Stretched out beneath him. Towering above him. Moaning and sighing, mouth open, eyes fluttering. Undulating—cresting. Falling into each other's arms.

Laughing together, teasing, gazing into each other's eyes.

Patrick whispering those words that he knew if Patrick said them, they would be true.

His chest ached. His longing for a man he barely knew was overwhelming him. The hatred had subsided. Patrick didn't act like someone who was a liar. He was open and honest-hearted. He wouldn't have it in him—to deceive someone like that. To knowingly hook up with a cheater.

Charles scrolled through his email. He was being discharged tomorrow. He had a lot to catch up on at the winery, but he was looking forward to going back to work.

The traction had come off the week before. His arm cast, a couple of weeks before that. Walking had been difficult at first. He'd be going to a physiotherapist and using a cane for a couple of months until his muscles regained their strength.

He set his phone on his chest.

His mind wandered back to Patrick. If he'd stuck with his courses, Patrick would be well on his way to becoming a Certified Sommelier by now. He'd know enough to start working for him.

Charles gripped his bedrail and adjusted his position.

Not that it mattered. Patrick would likely never set foot in his winery again. He wished Patrick would put aside the uncomfortable tension between them. Having an opportunity to mentor Patrick would give him a chance to get to know him better. And he desperately wanted that.

Discharge day rolled around. He'd need to call a cab, but at ten in the morning sharp, a figure graced the doorway; a goofy grin, a shopping bag, and a bottle of wine in one hand.

It was a face he'd been dreaming of seeing.

"What are you doing here?" Charles asked.

Patrick waggled the wine bottle. "I'm here to spring you. I heard you were going home today."

"Heard. How?"

The nurse walked into the room. "Your boyfriend here has been phoning every day to check on you. It's unfortunate he was out of town all this time. Came home just in time."

"Right, yeah." Charles nodded his head. "Back-to-back business trips."

"So tedious." Patrick walked over to the bed. "Thought they would never end."

"I dreamed of them wrapping up early."

"Me too."

A warmth spread through Charles' gut. So much undertone to their words. He had been miserable all those weeks not knowing if he'd ever see Patrick again. Worse; only seeing him from across the room in a busy crowd. Now Patrick was here … and he had no idea how to react.

Patrick threw the shopping bag onto the bed. "Sweats and a hoodie. Figured the accident wiped out your clothes. I had a few things laying around that'll bring out the color in your eyes."

He smirked as Charles peered into the bag.

"Couture, of course," Patrick added, then snorted.

"Thanks." Charles hauled the well-worn clothes out of the bag. Patrick had even thrown in a pair of old sneakers. He caught Patrick's eye. Patrick was enjoying this. Bringing Charles clothes that Patrick knew would make Charles cringe.

The nurse left them alone.

"Are you driving me home?" Charles asked.

"That's the idea. They filled me in on what to expect with your recovery. They think we live together. I may have given them that impression."

"My house *is* big enough for two."

"Figured."

"I'll be sleeping in the guest bedroom downstairs for a while."

"Easy access?"

"Ground floor."

"A burglar could come in and steal your innocence."

"He'd have a hard time finding it."

Patrick smiled. "Oh, my … spicy."

"Only if you taste it."

Patrick burst out laughing. Charles grinned. The back and forth they had was so natural—easy. He'd never had that with anyone before.

Charles slipped off the bed and untied the strings on his gown, then held it in place. He glared at Patrick who was yet again staring at him. "Do you mind?"

"Don't know what the big deal is." Patrick turned around. "I've already seen it."

"True. And I believe you owe me a rain check."

"I'll get right on that after I pull out my own wisdom teeth."

"Fewer teeth *would* make a more comfortable ride."

"In your dreams."

Wasn't that the truth.

The sweatpants were comfortable; thick and soft. He opted to keep on his hospital underwear. No need to go commando under Patrick's watchful eye. He pulled the university hoodie on over his head. It fit well enough. The ensemble was no different from the loungewear he wore at home. Just older and less stylish. It would do to get him home.

Out in the parking lot, Charles was confronted by what Patrick considered a road-worthy vehicle. He clambered into the passenger seat and placed the cane between his legs. He was surprised he couldn't see the pavement below the floorboards.

He hoped the truck had heating. Patrick had forgotten to bring him a coat. It was late October. The start of the cold season. The only thing saving him was the sun streaming across his body.

Patrick started the truck and began backing out of the parking spot.

Charles' hand flew out and gripped Patrick's arm.

"Stop!"

It had come on fast. The terror. Memories of the accident careened through his mind. The gut-wrenching sounds, the shock, the disorienting spin—the pain.

"It's all right." Patrick shifted the truck into park. "We can take this slow."

"Just give me a second."

"I've got all the seconds you need."

Charles looked into Patrick's eyes. So much patience was being exuded by them. Patience and affection. It was stunning. "Where did you come from?"

"Born and raised in Lake Country." Patrick smiled. "Should we try again?" He eased the truck back, then headed for the street. "Where am I going? I don't know your address."

"Just head up Gordon and wind your way to the top. I'll direct you."

"Oh … fancy. Lake view?"

"My back wall is all windows. You can't miss the lake."

"I'll have to check that out someday."

Charles relaxed in his seat. When Patrick wasn't shifting gears, he was offering Charles his hand. He'd been apprehensive to take it at first until he convinced himself it was simply a friendly gesture. The warmth and grip offered by Patrick's hand soothed him. When they pulled into his driveway, Charles was reluctant to release his hold on it.

Patrick gave Charles' hand a gentle squeeze, surrendered it, then turned off the engine.

"Do you need help to the door?"

"No … I can manage."

Come in with me. Please.

"We should exchange numbers."

"Good idea."

You won't need my number if you follow me inside.

"In case you need anything," Patrick said.

I need you now. I need you to hold me.

"I should be fine."

Charles looked down at his keys. It was obvious they had been in an accident. The pink leather fob was dirty and scuffed on one side. They passed their phones to each other and typed in their numbers. Charles smiled. Patrick had listed himself as Prancing Pony Boy.

"Can you wait until I get inside?" Charles asked.

"Sure."

Charles remained in his seat, staring at Patrick. There was a moment when he thought they might kiss. They'd certainly been working up to one with the innuendos behind their words earlier.

He turned away. There was a strong possibility he'd misread Patrick's intentions despite every damned thing Patrick had said to him. He refused to make a move and risk being rejected, foolishly believing Patrick saw something in him. It would be too humiliating.

He climbed out of the car, reached back, and grabbed his

cane. After he slammed the truck door, he hobbled up the driveway. He unlocked his front door, impressed the key worked.

He turned back.

Patrick waved at Charles from his truck, then rolled down his window, and stuck his head out through it. "Hey, is that job still a thing?"

"Are you working on those courses?"

"Ninety-eight-point nine percent so far."

"See, I knew you had in you. Come see me in my office in the morning. We'll get you set up."

"Already?"

"You're doing well. That's good enough for me."

"No interview?"

"I know everything I need to about you."

"Not everything." Patrick winked at him. "I have secrets."

Charles chuckled. "If I wait long enough, you'll probably blurt them out."

"Not entirely untrue."

"Okay, I'm tired. Thanks for the ride."

"Oh, man … you just walked straight into that one."

"Go ahead then. Say it."

Patrick smirked. "You think that ride was something? You ain't seen nothing yet."

Charles groaned as he shut the door behind him. Patrick was relentless in teasing him. Or maybe that was his thing, dropping sexual hints for attention. Either way, his cock was straining against his hospital-supplied underwear. The prospect of tasting Patrick's mouth had set it off.

He looked around his front entry.

The house had never felt emptier.

Charles glanced around his office. It was good to be back. His temporary replacement hadn't messed up his space too badly. He could spend the morning moving stuff around back to the way he liked things. He was going to keep his duties light today. He'd dive back in tomorrow.

He sat in the chair behind his desk. He was waiting for a knock on his door. Patrick had texted to say he'd be there by eight. Another fifteen minutes.

He didn't have to wait.

Charles straightened up as Patrick rapped on the door and walked in.

"You're early," he said.

Patrick smiled. "I barely slept. You have no idea how exciting this is for me."

"Sure. Butter up the boss on the first day."

Patrick smirked and snorted. "You sure have a habit of walking into innuendos."

"Maybe I meant to."

"Maybe I'll take you up on that." Patrick leaned on the back of a chair facing Charles' desk. He met Charles' gaze. There was purpose in the way Patrick was looking at him.

Charles steadied his breathing. He thought about locking his door and investigating the depth of desire burning in Patrick's eyes. He decided it would be inappropriate.

He cleared his throat and looked down at the employee welcome package.

"Here." Charles handed it to Patrick. "This is for you. There are a few forms to fill out, but you can do that during your lunch break."

"Where do I take this lunch break?"

"There's an employee break room."

"Doesn't sound like much fun."

"Not meant to be. But you'll find everyone is very friendly."

"Can I have lunch in here with you?"

Charles' heart leaped in his chest. As always, Patrick was being direct. But what did the request mean? His breath turned ragged as he perused Patrick's entire presence. He had dressed appropriately today, with cream pants, a black shirt, and his beard and mustache neatly trimmed.

"I don't think that would be wise?"

Patrick tipped his head. "You scared of me?"

Terrified.

It was warped, it really was, lusting after his ex-partner's ex-boyfriend.

They needed to keep things professional.

"Let's get you started." Charles grabbed his cane and lead the way out through his door. "Cindy is going to train you. Listen to everything she tells you. She's been here nine years. She knows her stuff. And she's patient." Charles smiled. "And a little bit wacky. We love Cindy around here."

"It says a lot about you. Her being here nine years."

"You'll find we treat our employees well. Everyone is integral to keeping this ship moving forward. Every single person is of tremendous value."

"It'll be nice to be appreciated for a change."

Charles turned to face Patrick. The words in his mind were tickling his tongue. They would send a strong signal. He wasn't sure he wanted to do that.

Oh, hell ... why not?

"Rest assured." He looked Patrick up and down. "I appreciate the hell out of you."

Patrick smirked. "Nicely done. You leaped right on that one."

"I had a good teacher."

Patrick shook his head. "God damned ... the things I could teach you."

Charles blushed, right through his entire face including his ears. "You can put that backpack in the staff room." He was having trouble even swallowing.

Patrick followed Charles and stuffed his backpack into a locker.

Charles cleared his throat. "I'll introduce you to Cindy?"

"Lead the way."

Charles took Patrick out to the tasting room. "This is where you'll spend most of your time. There's always some work to be done in the back as well. Organizing supplies and product."

Cindy bounded toward them. "This the newest victim?"

Charles chuckled. "You be nice to him. He's green but he has potential. Walk him through the entire wine list. Give him enough time to memorize it all before you put him on the floor."

"I'm one step ahead of you," Patrick said. "While *not* sleeping last night, I went on your website and reviewed everything in your product line. I'll still need to learn some nuances. Qualities of each wine. History. Why ours is better than all the other wineries."

"We tend to let the taster determine that on their own," Cindy said. "You're certainly going to save me some time.

I'll train you in cash as well. Sometimes the till gets pretty busy."

Charles clapped his hand on Patrick's back. "You ready for this?"

"Like I said before … dream job. I'm all over it."

And Patrick spoke the truth. He was born to work in a winery tasting room. His experience on the tour boats came in handy. He had people laughing and lingering—and buying. Patrick was a great salesperson, convincing people to buy full boxes rather than a few bottles.

Every time Charles came out to check, Cindy gave him a thumbs-up.

He leaned against the wall and watched Patrick for a while. Even his ridiculous bun didn't bother him so much anymore. Having his hair down would be a little too casual—even for Patrick.

Patrick turned and caught him staring. He gave Charles a smirk and a seductive wink.

It just about undid Charles.

Patrick had sent out a clear signal. This had moved beyond simple teasing. His chest rose and fell in anticipation; his fingers and toes tingling. This was going to happen.

Patrick's lips would be on his before the day was out.

Chapter Eleven | Patrick

It was his dream job, and he was excelling at it. Patrick loved the back-and-forth with the customers. It kept him engaged, and he enjoyed talking—sharing his knowledge. Some less-developed palettes were looking for a bottle of wine that would pair well with certain meats in their dinner plans. Some wanted to discuss the qualities of each wine in detail. He felt reasonably confident doing that. He thought he had it down. It felt like he'd always worked there.

He loved it.

Patrick looked over his shoulder. Charles was watching him again with more than a casual gaze that an employer would give his employee. Patrick smirked and winked at him.

He could sense the ripple of desire move through Charles' body.

This was going to happen.

Charles' lips would be on his before the day was out.

Charles walked toward him, cane in hand. He looked incredibly sexy with it. It gave him an air of distinction. "Can I see you in the staff room please?" Charles asked.

Patrick shivered and an ache spread through his gut. His breathing changed, the hunger for Charles building. He was quick on Charles' heels in his retreat to the staff room.

As soon as the door closed, Charles released his cane with a clatter, pressed Patrick against the wall, and attacked his mouth. His lips were everything Patrick had dreamed of.

Full, hot—wet.

Charles' approach was ferocious. Patrick submitted fully to him. Charles gripped Patrick's arms and slammed Patrick's hands above his head, crossed at the wrists.

So hot.

Charles backed off and pressed his teeth to his bottom lip as he studied Patrick. He growled, then found Patrick's mouth again. Patrick's knees almost failed him. Charles slipped his tongue into Patrick's mouth like it was on a desperate quest. The intensity found its way to Patrick's cock.

Charles stepped closer to him and pressed his thigh between Patrick's legs. With each kiss, Charles ground his leg against Patrick's cock. Charles' cologne wafted seductively around them.

Fuck.

Patrick tipped his face to break the contact with Charles' lips. In the state he was in, Patrick only wanted one thing. "Fuck me," he whispered.

Charles pressed his forehead to Patrick's, breathing heavily.

"Swear to me you didn't know Aubrey was still with me."

"I would never lie to you."

And he wouldn't. He would never lie to this man. Deceive him in any way. Do anything that made Charles feel unsure. Anything to make him feel unsafe.

"I hope you have condoms in that backpack of yours," Charles said.

Patrick slipped away from Charles' grasp. "I came prepared." He dashed over to the lockers, found his backpack, and dug around in it. He produced a condom and a small packet of lube.

"Back room." Charles pulled Patrick to him and took the condom from him. He grasped Patrick's hand and led him to a door in the back of the staff room.

Once inside, Charles switched on a light and shut the door.

The thickly walled portion of the log structure surrounded them. Rows upon rows of boxes of glasses. Patrick trembled. He'd never wanted a man as much as he wanted Charles. The urge was erupting from his very soul. He wanted Charles on his lips, on his skin—deep inside.

Charles turned Patrick to face the wall with rough hands. It was hot—so fucking hot the way Charles was taking charge. He couldn't help but wonder if he'd been this way with Aubrey. So commanding, so rugged—so virile. It was in stark contrast to his elegant looks.

Charles's dominant side was winding Patrick up. He hadn't realized how much he had been craving someone in charge. Without a second thought, his trust in Charles erupted.

Charles pressed Patrick's chest to the wall using his own chest against Patrick's back. Charles wrapped his arms around Patrick's hips, his hands searching for a way into Patrick's pants. He eventually released the button and fly and hauled Patrick's pants off his hips onto his thighs.

Charles' breath was hot across Patrick's neck and the back of his ear.

"Say it again," Charles demanded.

Patrick knew exactly what he meant. "Fuck me ... I want you to fuck me."

"How hard?"

Fuck.

"Hard. Fuck me hard."

Patrick could feel Charles lowering his dress pants. The buckle brushed across his ass as Charles released it. Charles kissed Patrick's neck then sucked and bit at his flesh. Patrick tipped his head to one side, giving Charles greater access. Charles latched on, humming against his skin.

It was sure to leave a mark.

The thought excited Patrick. He felt like he was being claimed.

"Hand me the lube," Charles whispered in his ear.

Patrick ripped open the packet with his teeth and passed it back to Charles. His heart hammered in his chest as he waited for Charles to get sorted and ready.

Then he felt it. Charles caressed his lubed cock past his cheeks and pressed against his hole. He held his breath as Charles pushed forward. The burn overtook everything. Blurred his mind.

Charles was big.

Ass thrashing big.

"Holy fuck." The words barely escaped his lips. Patrick placed his forehead on the log wall and concentrated on his breathing. He shifted his legs as far apart as his dropped pants would allow and tipped his ass back. Charles slid in and grasped both of Patrick's hips.

Patrick groaned and slammed his hand on the wall.

Charles was going to ride him hard and deep. Charles retreated and slid back home. A gust of exhalation burst from Patrick's chest. He was going to feel this for the rest of the day.

That thought made him smile.

Charles slammed his hips against Patrick's ass, rocking him against the wall time and again. Each thrust was glorious. More than he'd imagined. Patrick placed both hands on the wall and pushed back against Charles' cock. He wanted it deep. He wanted to feel it in his gut.

Patrick mewled and sighed, his throat erupting with sound every time Charles closed in against him. He reached back and grabbed Charles' hip, encouraging him to really let him have it.

Harder.

Charles nearly lifted Patrick off his feet as he drilled him. He started hammering faster. Patrick felt like he could cum any second. Charles was skilled. He was scraping the hell out of his gland.

Patrick closed his eyes. He could feel the intensity building in the man behind him.

Any moment now.

There it was.

Charles grunted in Patrick's ear then stiffened and held his cock in place in his ass. Then pumped it slowly in undulating thrusts filling the condom. Charles's body stilled and he wrapped his arms around Patrick's waist and embraced him for a second. He kissed the back of Patrick's neck and held his lips there. Then Charles spun Patrick around and struggled to his knees.

Patrick tipped his head back against the wall, shivering with deep, unprecedented longing as Charles sucked his cock into his mouth. He ran his hands into Charles' hair as Charles bobbed in place, his warm mouth and tongue sucking and licking. Charles backed off and sucked on the tip of Patrick's cock then ran his tongue around the thick ridge, then dove back on.

Patrick looked down at Charles. The next time Charles backed off, Patrick reached down and lifted Charles' face by tipping up his chin.

Just so he could look at him.

It was a sight he'd dreamed of.

Charles on his knees, pleasuring him.

He released Charles' face and Charles sunk back onto his cock. There was affection in the way he sucked and released. Charles lifted Patrick's cock to press against his belly and licked the underside then pulled one of Patrick's balls into his mouth. He dragged it down hard, his tongue dancing across the aching sack. Charles left it wet and warm, then dove back on his cock.

Patrick gripped Charles' hair. He was close.

Charles retreated again and used his hand to pump Patrick's length. He tickled the slit with his tongue then jammed Patrick's cock right to the back of his throat.

He sucked hard, his tongue gliding back and forth.

It was too much. Patrick closed his eyes and came hard. Pumping burst after burst down Charles' throat. He fucked Charles' face with each pulse until his body calmed.

Charles sucked him to the end of his length, then dropped Patrick's cock from his mouth. He looked up at Patrick and smiled. "Can you help me up? Practically an invalid."

Patrick smirked, grasped Charles' outstretched hand, and pulled.

Charles rose to his feet. Patrick grabbed his face and kissed him. Charles took control and dove deeper. He pressed Patrick against the wall and subdued him. He slipped his tongue into Patrick's mouth. Patrick tangled with it, then pushed his tongue into Charles' mouth. He wanted to taste everything. Everything they had done together. Everything he had left behind.

Charles moaned as Patrick explored his mouth.

When they finally separated, they were both panting.

"That was amazing," Patrick whispered. "I knew it would be … but wow."

"You've been thinking about it?"

"You've invaded my dreams completely."

"You've plagued mine. I knew you'd be delicious."

"It's my diet."

Charles snorted out a laugh.

Patrick fiddled with pulling his pants back up and fastened them as Charles did the same with his dress pants after peeling off the condom. He buried it under some paper in a garbage can.

"My place tonight?" Charles said.

Patrick grinned. "Do I get to see the lake?"

"I think you'll be too distracted."

Charles wandered back to Patrick and gave him a slow, sultry kiss. The kind you felt in your toes. The kind that said Charles would be gentler with him tonight.

"I didn't mean for it to be like that," Charles said after releasing Patrick's mouth. "I imagined asking you out for dinner. Having a bottle of wine. Inviting you back to my place. Taking you to my bedroom. Drawing every one of those incredible noises you make out of you."

"You can still do that. I'd love to have dinner with you."

"Then it's a date." Charles licked his lips.

"God, I love when you do that." Patrick placed his finger on Charles' bottom lip. Then leaned forward and captured Charles' mouth. He hummed against his lips. They tasted like heaven.

Eventually, he had to relinquish them.

"Get back to work," Charles said and smacked Patrick's ass as Patrick turned to open the door.

Patrick smirked. "So demanding."

"You have no idea."

Patrick felt that answer in his cock. Exactly what was he getting himself into? He wandered back to his station behind the serving bar. He was so game for whatever it was.

He would follow wherever Charles led him.

The rest of the day seemed to stretch on forever. His shift ended at five, but he agreed to work until seven because

Charles told him he wouldn't be finished until then. Charles had made reservations for seven thirty at a restaurant Patrick never would have been able to afford. Aubrey had never even taken him to it. But then Aubrey preferred if they stayed home.

More control over him that way. Now he knew what Aubrey had been working up to.

Why am I thinking about Aubrey?

Patrick wiped the countertop. He knew why. Because he'd been intimate with a man Aubrey had spent seven years with. They'd likely done all kinds of sexual things together. He wasn't sure if that made him nervous or if it turned him on. How had he compared to Aubrey?

Charles stepped up behind him. A respectable distance, but close enough that Patrick could hear Charles' heavy breathing. He was turned on. "What are you thinking about?"

Patrick turned to face him. "You. I can still feel you."

Charles gave him a shy smile. "I can still taste you."

Patrick groaned and reached for Charles' arm. He was sure to keep the touch discreet. Cindy was busy with a customer at the till. He squeezed Charles' arm. "Can we get out of here now?"

"I'll meet you at the restaurant." Charles looked at Cindy who was boxing up bottles and chatting with the customer. "We can't be seen leaving in the same car."

That made Patrick feel a little deflated, but it was understandable. They weren't an item. They'd fucked and were going on their first date. The staff at Quail's Run didn't need to know they had an interest in each other and a history beyond Charles meeting Patrick at a wine tasting.

That's what Charles had told everyone. That they'd started chatting at the summer event and he had discovered Patrick was quite knowledgeable. Charles had promised Patrick a job once Patrick completed some courses. He had thought Patrick would be a great addition to the team.

No one needed to know they had Aubrey in common.

Most of the staff would have been around for that fallout. When Aubrey dumped Charles. The thought of Charles going through that reminded Patrick of his own encounter with Aubrey leaving him on the curb. He studied the intensity of Charles' gaze, studying his eyes.

How anyone could let this talented, intelligent, beautiful man go—he couldn't understand.

"I want to kiss you again," Patrick whispered.

"Soon." Charles wet his lips. "Go. I'll meet you there."

"You have a car?"

"No, I'll catch a cab."

Patrick nodded. "Okay. See you there. I'll order a bottle."

It felt strange pulling away from the winery without Charles. What they'd shared had been intense. Months of pent-up attraction had ignited in a crude frenzy of desire.

It had been pure lust.

Maybe tonight, they would slow things down a bit. Really explore each other. Patrick gripped his steering wheel. He wanted to taste every square inch of that man.

He pulled into a parking lot and found his way to the restaurant.

"Charles Avery. Party of two."

The host nodded. "Ah, with Charles, yes. Follow me, please." As they walked the host got chatty. "How is he? We heard about his accident. We were all worried about him."

"He's healing … feeling much better."

Of course, the restaurant knew Charles. Patrick looked around at the other diners. He felt underdressed. Charles had lent him a white button-up shirt, tie, and jacket but they didn't match the unsophisticated style of his pants or his shoes. He sat on the chair that was pulled out for him.

His face flushed crimson. What the hell was Charles doing with him? He didn't belong in this world. This was beyond what Aubrey had even introduced him to. The white tablecloths, the real candles, and floral arrangements at each table. His stomach churned as he considered leaving.

Then he saw him.

And smiled.

Charles.

He remembered what he was doing there.

"Hey, you're here," Charles said, sounding a little surprised, as he sat in his chair.

"Where else did you expect me to be?"

Charles shook his head. "I don't know. Thought you might be done with me now that we've done the deed. If you're feeling that way—no offense if you decide to leave."

Oh my god. What?

"Jesus … what the hell did Aubrey do to you?" Patrick moved his foot forward under the table until he made contact with Charles' shoe. "I have no intention of leaving."

The look of distrust on Charles' face was startling. This man needed more than just their shoes touching. He reached across the table and lay his hand palm up in front of Charles.

Charles furrowed his brow but placed his hand in Patrick's. Patrick closed his fingers around Charles' hand. Charles' skin was warm and smooth with a few callouses at the base of his fingers. He wasn't a man that had never done manual labor. Patrick wondered what his past looked like.

"I have no plans to ditch you," Patrick said.

Charles slipped his hand from Patrick's.

"I'm not looking for anything."

Patrick placed his hand on his lap. "Sure, I get it, but we've only just started this. I'll totally back off if you need me to, but can we at least see where it goes?"

Charles looked down. "I couldn't stand to go through another breakup."

Whoa. Back up.

"That's why you're not looking for anything? Because you think it'll end in a breakup?"

Charles raised his head. "That's what always happens."

Patrick leaned back in his chair and crossed his arms. "Oh, my god. You had no intention of even giving us a chance, did you? You were going to walk away from me before we even started anything serious. Tonight, was going to be it, wasn't it? A little fun … then take off."

"It's for the best."

"How do you know what's best for me? Maybe I have serious feelings for you. What are you going to do with that? Just discard me without even giving us an opportunity to build something because I might break your heart someday. How do you know this is destined to end?"

"It always does."

"So, you've had a bit of bad luck with relationships. I have too."

"Why did you have sex with me?"

"Because you're fucking hot …"

"See. That's all it ever is."

"Let me finish." Patrick propped himself on the edge of the table with his elbows. "Because you're fucking hot and crazy amazing. Smart, witty, and deep. You're so bloody deep. You've turned my world upside down. I can't wait to find out more about you."

Charles frowned. "You're delusional."

Patrick pushed away from the table and almost stood up. Charles was pissing him off. The guy really believed he had nothing to offer.

"You're full of shit, but if you really are a lump of coal, I'll figure it out for myself. Don't tell me what I'm going to feel because you've already sucked me in. And it has little to do with your looks. Sure, that's what first attracted me. But that's the way it is with the start of most relationships. Don't you dare make me feel like my interest in you is flawed."

"My conviction about this is no reflection on you."

"Sure sounds like it. I'll have you know; I don't hang out with losers. And I certainly don't have sex with them." Patrick shrugged. "Aside from dating apps."

"Aubrey wasn't exactly stellar."

"He slipped through my radar ... and yours too."

Charles simply grunted.

Patrick picked up the drink menu. "Let's order some wine."

Charles followed Patrick's lead. "I'm in the mood for a Syrah."

"Then let's do that."

When the server approached, Charles ordered the bottle, and when presented with it, he went through the process of approving its quality. Patrick was intrigued by how Charles was taking the lead. He hoped it carried through to the rest of their night. He liked the commanding Charles.

Patrick sat back in his chair.

He had every intention of going through with this evening. The dinner date, the heading back to Charles's place—the sex. Every cell in his body wanted this man.

They were both poured a glass.

Patrick took a sip and set the glass down. "You have a lot to offer, Charles. Please believe that. Like I said this morning,

I would never lie to you."

Charles heaved out a sigh. "I've had it rough my whole life. My dad was never satisfied with anything I did." Charles met Patrick's gaze. "I tried so hard to please him. Everything I did was never good enough. My work wasn't good enough. My grades were never good enough. My looks just pissed him off and made him hate me more. I was the pretty sissy boy he never wanted."

Patrick set his glass down.

"Jesus, Charles … I had no idea."

"When I told him I was gay, that was the final straw. He disowned me. The guys I dated after that, confirmed what I knew. I was useless when it came to relationships. A long list of guys fucking and leaving me. When Aubrey came around, I thought I had found the one. He didn't discard me after a few months. He told me he loved me."

"I don't think Aubrey has the capability to truly love anyone."

"I know that now." Charles took a sip of his wine. He set the glass down. "He shredded my heart. I never want to go through that again."

Patrick reached forward and touched Charles' hand. "I can't promise things will work out between us. We barely know each other. But I can promise I'll be gentle with you. I give you my word, I'll try to be there with you until you realize what an amazing person you are."

"I don't know, Patrick. I want to believe you, I do."

"Then let's just see what happens, all right."

Charles nodded his head. "Okay. I'll think about it."

"Perfect." Patrick picked up the food menu. "What's good?"

"I'm having a steak."

"A red meat lover … liking it. See … we already have

things in common."

"That's hardly earth-shattering."

"So completely opposite of what happened this morning."

Charles smirked. "I thought they were going to hear you out in the tasting room. Good thing that room is practically soundproof."

Patrick sighed. Something was burning on his tongue. It was a question that had been playing on his mind all afternoon. "So, you've used that room before."

Charles hesitated. "Yes."

"Aubrey?"

"And others before him."

"Now I feel cheap." Patrick draped his napkin on his lap. The server came at the most inopportune time. They ordered their steaks. Rare—bloody.

"If it makes a difference, aside from Aubrey, you're the first one I've actually liked."

Patrick laughed. "Am I on a date with a slut?"

"I used to get around. Before Aubrey."

Charles needed to stop doing that. Bringing Aubrey into the conversation. It reminded him of how bizarre this was—having sex and going on a date with his ex-boyfriend's ex.

"Let's stop mentioning his name. It makes me feel oogie."

Charles laughed. "Oogie?"

"Yeah. Creeped out."

"It is a little weird, isn't it? Us doing this together."

"I keep feeling like the relationship police are going to pull up on me."

"They'd discover you're a good driver."

"Not just with my car," Patrick said.

"I like letting someone else drive."

"Wouldn't have suspected that."

"Sometimes it's nice to be a passenger."

Patrick shifted in his seat. "Fuck, you're making me hot."

"You already are."

The return of the sexual banter was invigorating. Charles was feeling more comfortable again. He studied Charles across the table. He was finishing his first glass. He wondered if Charles had let him into his secret vault about his past or if he shared intimate details of his life with everyone.

"Who else knows?" Patrick blurted out. He couldn't help himself.

"Knows what?"

"About your past."

"I don't generally share it." Charles filled his glass. "He who shall not be named knows. But not in great detail. He never seemed very interested."

"I'm interested. Tell me more."

"Okay." Charles took a sip of his wine. "I had five relationships before Aubrey. All of them ended in less than a month because the guys got bored with me."

"How do you know that? Maybe they just weren't the right person."

"Three of them told me they were bored. One of them told me I was a pretty face, but they didn't want to go beyond that. The other one ghosted me."

"Fuck, Charles. That wasn't your fault. Sounds like they were all assholes."

"Maybe—but it didn't do much for my confidence." Charles sighed and leaned back in his chair. "Can I be honest with you?"

"Always."

"I'm terrified by you."

The steaks arrived. Again, a badly timed interruption. The

entire dish looked amazing. Mashed potatoes with chives atop, a mixed medley of root vegetables, and pools of pink liquid with a slab of luscious-looking meat at its center. It would have to wait.

"Why?" Patrick asked. "What makes me so scary?"

"I spent so much time hating you. It's permanently burned into my brain. There's a battle happening up there. Because I'm attracted to you."

"I'm having the same battle."

"How do we get past that?"

Patrick ran his fork through his potatoes. "Time."

Charles nodded. "This steak is getting cold, but I'd like to keep this conversation going later. Maybe tonight." He looked up at Patrick. "Or maybe in the morning."

Patrick smirked. "Are you inviting me for a sleepover?"

"Yes. One without the obligatory pajamas and silly boy talk."

Patrick cut into his steak. "There's only one boy I want to talk about. Word has it, I'm quite smitten with him. He gives me shivers." Patrick winked at Charles. "And makes my cock hard."

Charles groaned. "Finish your steak. I want to get you out of here."

Chapter Twelve | Charles

Charles couldn't work the lock on his front door fast enough. The whole trip home, Patrick had been winding him up, caressing his cock through his pants out of sight of the cab driver.

They tumbled through the door together. Coats were ripped off, and lips sought each other out every chance they got. They stumbled through the entry into the living room.

Patrick pulled away and wandered over to the wall of windows.

"Holy shit. You can see everything from here. The lake—the entire city." Patrick looked down to the ground below. "And you have a pool."

"And a hot tub."

"Nice. Maybe I'll *take* you in that later."

Anywhere. Anytime.

After the positive response from Patrick upon revealing so much about his life, he'd let that man do anything. Charles wandered up to Patrick and leaned in close to his lips.

"You can *take* me anywhere."

Patrick hummed and began to unbutton Charles' shirt. "Right now, I want you naked."

A demand.

It was what he needed. A break from being in charge.

Charles stepped back, set his cane against the sofa, and removed his shirt. He unlatched his belt, button, and fly, and let his pants drop to the floor. He kicked them away from his feet and played with the band of his underwear to tease Patrick.

"All of it," Patrick said.

Charles held Patrick's gaze and licked his lips. When he got the groan he was looking for, he stripped off his socks, then hooked his thumbs in his underwear. His cock was hard and straining to be released from the thin fabric. He pulled them down slowly and tossed them to one side.

"Oh ... fuck." Patrick walked over to Charles and ran his hand across Charles' chest and brushed each of his nipples with his thumb. The sensation was electric like Patrick possessed a cattle prod. He felt every caress right through to his cock.

"Where is your bedroom?"

Charles cleared his throat. "Guest room for now. Just down the hall."

"Perfect." Patrick followed Charles down a short hallway to a set of double doors.

It was elaborate, the guest room. Everything in his house was elaborate. Charles was paid well at the winery, plus he'd inherited his father's winery and sold it. He could afford nice things.

"Wow ... sweet." Patrick wandered into the room. He stopped at the foot of the bed and gave Charles a once-over. "Even sweeter." He patted the bed. "Need you on here."

It seemed Patrick was going to continue driving.

Charles could handle that.

He crawled to the head of the bed, adjusted a pillow, and lay down. He laced his hands behind his head as Patrick stripped off his clothes. Patrick's lean body extended to his groin, the v-cut that led to his cock smooth and sublime. He'd had an intimate introduction to the region earlier in the day, but seeing the whole package of Patrick's body lit by bedroom lights had him squirming with longing. He wanted that body all over and inside him—flesh to flesh.

Patrick joined him on the bed. He started with a kiss on the center of Charles' chest. Then Patrick reached up and undid the tie holding his hair. It cascaded down onto his shoulders like a blond mane, framing his face. The word *ethereal* danced in Charles' mind.

Patrick smiled down at him.

Something unknotted inside Charles' chest. Patrick looked like one of those men you might see on the cover of a romance novel. The hero of the story. He cupped Patrick's cheek and brought him down to his lips. Kiss after kiss, his heart swelled. They'd only just started their story.

Charles was eager to discover what might happen next.

"I thought about it," Charles said.

Patrick smiled. "Thought about what?"

"Us."

"And what did you decide? Is there going to be an *us*?"

"I'd like there to be."

Patrick grabbed Charles' face and gave him a crushing kiss. He pulled away but kept Charles' face in his hands. "I knew you couldn't walk away from what we've started."

Charles' stroked his fingers through Patrick's hair and lifted away the strands shielding his face. "I love your hair. Didn't think I would but it suits you."

"Plus, it comes in handy."

Patrick lay another kiss on Charles' chest. This time Patrick's hair brushed across Charles' skin. His chest, his nipples, his ribcage. The sensation was seductive and exhilarating. Combined with the feel of Patrick's facial hair, Charles breathed up into the experience.

A kiss at the crest of his ribcage.

His belly.

One hip then the next.

Down his thigh.

Patrick stopped and ran his finger down the long scar on his outer thigh that extended from just below his hip to above his knee. The surgical site where they had repaired his broken femur.

Then Patrick kissed his knee and dropped dots of kisses down his shin. Charles' cock was eager and tight. Patrick's hair had dragged across it, thrilling it.

The top of his foot—a kiss.

Patrick sucked each of Charles' toes into his mouth, playing the tip of his tongue across them. Across to the next foot. His toes. The top of his foot—up his shin.

By the time Patrick reached Charles' lips, Charles was undulating and groaning, grinding his cock into the air, his ass clenching and releasing. The caring attention Patrick had bestowed on him had been erotic and maddeningly inadequate.

"Condoms?" Patrick asked.

"Bedside drawer—to the right—there." Charles pointed.

Patrick came back with a bottle of lube and a couple of purple packets. Charles licked his lips as Patrick rolled on the condom. Patrick had a beautiful cock—long and lean, like him.

Charles bent his knees and let his legs fall open. Patrick started with a warm, lubed thumb. He wasn't fooling around—or wasting time. Charles closed his eyes and rode the emotion of being cared for. So soon in—his trust in Patrick was unprecedented.

Patrick's thumb was replaced as Patrick towered above him. Charles wrapped his legs around Patrick's waist as Patrick eased his way inside his body. Charles gazed up at him—a gentle, passionate face amidst tresses of blond hair. His heart tripped inside his chest.

This is what it was supposed to be like. Your lover looking down at you with affection, intent on fulfilling your pleasure. Meeting your needs above his own.

"You all right?" Patrick checked in with him before withdrawing his initial thrust.

Tears threatened to form in Charles' eyes.

This is what love was supposed to feel like.

Charles simply nodded, afraid that if he spoke, his voice would crack with emotion. He closed his eyes as Patrick retreated and plunged. He wrapped his legs tighter around Patrick. His arms embraced the man that was drawing so much out of him. So much hope—maybe even joy.

He managed a, "Go slow," without betraying his state of mind.

"For you—anything." Patrick kissed him. The rock of his hips was steady and unhurried. Patrick gathered Charles up in his arms, one hand behind his neck, the other behind his back.

"You're safe with me," Patrick whispered in his ear.

Charles couldn't stop them. Tears welled up in his eyes, then released onto his cheeks. Patrick simply kissed the wet streaks and whispered, "I've got you."

Each stroke of Patrick's cock had intent. It dragged across where it needed to, tender and capable. His hair danced across Charles' cheeks and shoulders, and forehead, creating a screen. A curtain to protect them from the world. Patrick kissed him, long and slow.

Charles felt like he was floating.

Patrick buried his face against Charles' neck. Their chests layered. He increased the pace of his hips, grunting and sighing in Charles' ear. Patrick clung tight to him. A soft, "You mean so much to me," and then he came, his body jerking and thrusting until he was finally still.

Charles threw his hands over his eyes as Patrick slipped down his body and took his cock into his mouth. He had never—absolutely never experienced anything like what Patrick had just carried him through. He lowered his hands and dug his fingers into Patrick's hair. Patrick's whiskers were creating a whole new level of pleasure against his balls. It wasn't long until Charles crested.

He pulled Patrick up and into his arms. He needed to hold and be held by him.

Patrick kissed Charles' cheek as he snuggled into Charles' embrace.

"We fit, you and I," Patrick said. "In so many ways … we fit."

"You feel good in my arms. I know that for sure."

"What else do you know for sure in your life?" Patrick drew a line with his finger from Charles' ear down to the tip of his chin.

"That I'm good at my job. And I love it."

"And?"

Charles smiled. "That there's someone who thinks I'm worth getting to know."

"Someone who is crazy about you."

"I feel the same." Charles rolled until he was looking down at Patrick. He brushed the hair away from Patrick's face, then kissed him. He looked into Patrick's eyes. They were staring up at him with such wonder and affection. "You did something to me tonight."

Patrick brushed the back of his hand across Charles' cheek. "I felt it."

Charles shook his head. What he had felt with Patrick was beyond comprehension. "No one has ever made me feel that way."

"Cherished?"

That was it. That's what he'd felt. "Yes."

"It's what you deserve. You're a beautiful man—inside and out. I keep telling you. You have a lot to offer. And I want to find out every single thing about you."

Charles kissed Patrick's forehead. "Where did you come from?"

Patrick smirked as Charles pulled away. "I told you. Lake Country."

The next morning, Charles awoke entangled in Patrick's arms and legs. He decided to lie there for a while and enjoy the warm body beside him. They'd had sex again before falling asleep. Patrick on the bottom this time. He was glad Patrick was flexible that way. Aubrey had almost always made him bottom. Mostly on his hands and knees. Completely impersonal fucking.

What he'd experienced with Patrick was so much more than that. He'd felt revered and respected. Like he mattered. Patrick had made him feel truly desired for more than his body.

"Good morning." Patrick turned on his side and kissed Charles' shoulder.

"It is."

Patrick's hair was a mess of blond on his pillow. He looked good enough to eat. Charles glanced at the clock on his bedside table. They had a few minutes yet before they would have to get organized to head to work. Even figuring in showers and breakfast. Charles sat up, rolled, and straddled Patrick's hips. The position made his leg ache a bit, but he was willing to put up with it.

"Why, Mr. Avery." Patrick grinned. "Whatever are you intending to do to me?"

Charles took a hold of Patrick's cock and stroked it.

"My intentions are corrupt, I'm afraid."

Patrick clapped his hand over his mouth, trying not to laugh.

"How so?" he managed.

Charles grinned. "I plan to sit on your cock."

Patrick was having trouble keeping it together. "But won't that be uncomfortable?"

"Only for a moment, my dear … only for a moment. Then stars."

Patrick shrieked with laughter and pulled Charles down for a kiss. It was long and sensuous, and soul-rousing. He released Charles' face. "Proceed."

They were late for work.

Chapter Thirteen | Patrick

The sun was sinking below the horizon. He could see it from the expanse of windows in Charles' living room. It had been a week since their first sexual encounter and their admission of affection for each other. The rest of the week had been like a dream. Working together every day, then retreating to Charles' home—his safe space. Patrick had barely been home in days.

Patrick was learning slowly just how anxious Charles could be about so many things. It didn't turn him off. Quite the opposite. It endeared Charles to him. Charles was so commanding and confident at work. It was like getting a peek behind the curtain to see what it took to play that part.

He kissed the back of Charles' neck. They were embracing in front of the window. Patrick had Charles wrapped up in his arms, his chest to Charles' back. Friday night. It was the start of the weekend. Charles had taken Saturday off work, and they had plans to visit wineries tomorrow in the South Okanagan. Oliver, Osoyoos, and Naramata.

"I'm looking forward to tomorrow," Patrick said. "Aside from work and a few short walks, we haven't left your house much. It'll be nice to go out together."

"Groceries don't count?"

"Not when you get most of them delivered."

"I only like to go to the butcher to pick out my meat." Charles turned to face Patrick. "Maybe next time we're out, you can pick up some stuff from your apartment to keep here."

"That's moving a bit fast."

"Is it?" Charles kissed Patrick. There was so much longing in that kiss that Patrick was on the verge of breaking one of his own rules.

Don't move too fast.

Patrick pressed his hand to Charles' chest, breaking the kiss.

"Let's give it another couple of weeks." He'd been using a fresh toothbrush and deodorant from Charles' stockpile. Washed his work clothes once. Been back to his apartment to change the rest of the days. Spent a bit of time by himself at his own place. He had a lot to think about.

The truth was, he hadn't expected the relationship to go this far with Charles. An appreciation for each other. A bit of fun. Nothing more. In the last few days, something had changed. He wanted love in his life again, but what was happening with Charles was scaring him. The thought of extending his heart to another so soon after Aubrey had trampled on it made him apprehensive.

It was hard to resist the guy, though. He'd been on target about Charles' depth. He was a thinker. A ponderer. It was captivating. Everything about Charles was intriguing.

Spending so much time together, he could tell they had both developed some significant feelings for each other. The more Charles opened up to him, the closer he felt to the gentle, engaging man. All that aside, he wasn't sure he was ready.

"I'm sorry," Charles said. "I don't mean to push."

"Things have grown intense pretty quick."

"And that scares you."

"Doesn't it scare you?"

"I'm not sure." Charles shook his head. "I want you here with me."

Patrick sighed. Deep down, he wanted the same thing. Maybe he should stop fighting it. Take his own advice and see where their feelings for each other took them.

Time to change the subject.

"What winery are we going to start with tomorrow?"

The sigh of dejection from Charles due to the dismissal was visible. "I thought we'd start in Naramata. Work our way back around the lake."

"And you've hired a limo for this whole thing?"

"Neither of us will be in any state to drive by the time we're partway through."

"You don't do anything halfway, do you?" Patrick asked.

"Not when I have someone to share it with."

"Fuck, Charles. Why do you have to be so damned adorable and sexy all at once?" Patrick held Charles' face in his hands and kissed him. Every time their lips met; it was like coming home after a long trip away in a foreign country. It was where he was meant to be.

Patrick released Charles's mouth, pressed his forehead to Charles', and cupped the back of Charles' head. "A toothbrush, some underwear, and a clean work shirt. That's it."

Charles smiled. "I'll clear some space."

He hoped this wouldn't backfire—move too fast and throw everything off the rails. That was his experience. But his emotional connection with Charles was growing. If he was going to have faith in what was happening; that it was something worth moving ahead with, he was going to have to check his brain at the door and let his heart lead.

That terrified him.

Time for another subject change.

"What's for dinner?" he asked.

"That chicken cordon bleu we picked up is calling to me. Some broccoli and I have a noodle recipe that has been in my family forever."

"Like making them—noodles?"

"It's easy." Charles led the way into the kitchen. "Flour, milk, and eggs. Put it through a special press into boiling water. Fish them out when they're cooked. It's called spaetzle. German."

"Your mom?" Charles had already told him; his dad came from England. Immigrated a few years before Charles was born. He didn't talk about his mother much. She'd left when he was nine. Part of his hangup regarding not being good enough. She'd never contacted him after she left.

"Yeah, they met in Germany. Her ancestry is from Spain, though."

That would explain Charles' dark hair and olive skin tone that tanned up so beautifully. He wondered what Charles' family had looked like. What Charles had looked like as a child. Charles had told him he hadn't kept any pictures. That he'd burned them all. It was heartbreaking to hear Charles had tried to wipe out any existence of his family.

"Have you ever looked for her?" Patrick asked.

Charles turned on the oven to convection to preheat. "Why on earth would I do that? She abandoned me."

"You might get some closure if you talked to her."

"That's more likely to rip open old wounds."

Patrick gripped Charles' shoulders. "Those wounds are still open and weeping." Charles looked at the floor. Patrick raised Charles' face with a finger under Charles' chin. He gazed into Charles' eyes. "You're still bruised and battered. You're carrying the weight of that rejection."

Charles struggled away. "Why is this so important to you?"

"Why? Because you're important to me. I want you whole. I want the man I know is in there to emerge. That's the man I want to potentially fall in love with."

There he'd said it. So soon in, love was on his mind. He wasn't there yet, but all paths were leading in that direction. He was having trouble imagining life without Charles.

"You think that's where we're going?"

"I don't know for sure yet."

Charles nodded slowly and sighed. "Can you grab the broccoli and break out the florets?"

"You mean cut it?"

"That's what I said."

Patrick smirked. Sometimes Charles was so incredibly proper. He was keen to know more about Charles' upbringing. How had the elegant man wrestling with the oven rack come into being? He knew his dad had been hard on him. What or who else had influenced him?

"Do you have a favorite movie star?" Patrick asked as he chopped the broccoli.

Charles closed the oven door. "Always had a penchant for James Dean."

A *Rebel Without a Cause* fan. Nice.

"Marlon Brando for me if we're talking about the 50s."

"Favorite band?" Charles asked.

"Pink and Lady Gaga."

Charles laughed. "Predictable."

"What about you?"

"Eric Clapton," Charles answered.

Patrick decided to go off on a tangent. "Favorite color?"

"Purple. You?"

"Blue." Patrick smirked. "Okay, lying … pink again."

Charles crossed his arms and leaned against the counter. "Favorite sexual position?"

"I thought you would have figured that out. Missionary. I like to kiss you and see your eyes." He wandered up to Charles and put his arms around Charles' neck. "You?"

Charles kissed him. "Anything that involves you."

Patrick smiled. "Good answer."

"Noodles." Charles grabbed Patrick's ass and hauled him close. "Help me mix up the batter."

"That sounds dirty."

"Only if we spill it everywhere."

"Maybe we should mix up the batter in every room of this house."

"I'd like that … but right now, I'm hungry."

Patrick pouted. "No fun."

He scrapped the broccoli off the cutting board and into a pot of water Charles had placed on the stove. Charles pulled a large pot out of the cupboard, filled it with water, and turned the heat to high. From memory, Charles mixed up the noodle batter. When the water was boiling, he used a strange press contraption to squeeze strands of noodles into the water. While it was cooking, Charles placed a bowl, sieve, and slotted spoon on the counter.

Miraculously, everything came together in time. Charles was a good cook. Yet another gold star in his favor. The man continued to surprise him. Patrick wanted to know more.

"Favorite genre of book?" Patrick asked then shoveled a mouthful of chicken into his mouth.

Charles set his utensils down. "I don't read much anymore."

"But if you had to pick up a book, what would it be?"

"I like Elizabeth George. Any kind of mystery set in Britain."

That was surprising. He'd expected Charles to be into someone like Kurt Vonnegut.

They ate in silence for a few minutes. Everything was cooked to perfection. Every day with Charles, all their meals were beyond what he could whip up himself.

"Have you ever read any gay romance?" Patrick asked.

Charles furrowed his brow. "Is that a thing?"

"Of course, it's a thing. I'll introduce you to a few titles. Maybe I could read you the steamy bits aloud. Get you in the mood."

Charles smiled. "I'm always in the mood with you."

Patrick snorted and laughed.

"You're full of good answers this evening."

"Hard not to be." Charles reached for Patrick's hand across the table. Charles clung tightly to his. There was so much unsaid in that grip. It was gentle and caring, but it was also desperate; like Charles was afraid to let go. That if he did, Patrick might disappear.

"What do we want to watch on TV tonight?" Patrick broke the moment. It had become too intense. The way Charles had been looking at him—it had caused his breathing to cease. "I wouldn't mind checking out Brit Box. See if there are any of those British mysteries you like."

"Sounds perfect." Charles relinquished Patrick's hand and rose to clear the dishes. Patrick helped him load the dishwasher and wash up the pots and baking sheet. And that weird apparatus that had made the noodles. It turned out to be a beast to clean.

Charles poured them each a glass of wine then they retired to the living room. Patrick tucked his legs and curled up against Charles' side. He'd rarely felt this relaxed with anyone. He didn't have to put on an act around Charles. Play a part. They were just them—and they fit.

The murder mystery was entertaining enough. More than Patrick thought it would be. He'd watched a few in the past but never with an enthusiast. The exclamations, laughter, and outbursts of the possible *whodunnit* completed the surprisingly cozy experience.

But now it was late.

"Bed?" Patrick rose to his feet and held out his hand to Charles.

"Absolutely. Early start tomorrow. Drinking with breakfast at its finest." Charles accepted Patrick's help then retrieved his cane and followed Patrick down the hall.

The sex they'd been having each night had taken on a profound, intimate nature. The tenderness and care exuded by both men nearly brought them to tears. There was so much being unsaid in those moments. Even afterward when they clung to each other—silence.

It was there under the surface, growing—evolving. Patrick sighed as Charles brought him to climax. He'd said it before. They just fit. Two opposing cogs that found unity together.

Patrick brushed his hand along Charles' face as they lay face to face in bed.

"Do you know what I see in you?" he asked.

"Is this a trick question?"

"No." Patrick kissed him. "I see strength, courage, resilience, and integrity."

Charles' eyebrows rose but he didn't argue with him.

"Do you want to know what I see in you?"

"Tell me." Patrick moved closer so he could sling his leg over Charles' hip and tuck in close to him. Belly to belly. Cock to cock. Their breath mingled between them.

"Warmth, compassion, generosity, humor, and devotion."

"Devotion?"

It hadn't occurred to Patrick that Charles would have picked up on that. His devotion. It was so early in the game; it shouldn't be there. And yet, it was.

"Does that scare you? That I see that in you?" Charles asked.

Patrick held Charles' gaze. "It's too soon."

"I thought you said you wanted to see where this thing between us led?"

Charles was right. He had said that, but he hadn't expected to be pulled so deep—so quickly. His brain was throwing up blockades. His heart was not.

"It's too soon," he repeated.

Charles ran his fingers across Patrick's lips. "The devotion goes both ways."

Too fast. Too fast.

Patrick's heart raced. On the verge of panic. The only way he could think to make himself feel better was to envelop himself in Charles' arms. To have Charles hold him.

It was the one thing that would bring him any peace.

Patrick climbed into the back of the limo ahead of Charles. It was pure luxury. The tinted windows. The black leather seats. The bar with crystal glasses. The privacy screen.

Charles slid in across from him. Elegant and sophisticated. He was wearing the blue suit Patrick had admired Charles in the day he had walked into Quail's Run winery for the first time. His grey woolen peacoat was folded on the seat beside him. He was pure class.

Patrick looked down at his own clothes. Khaki pants, a worn parka, and hiking boots. Charles adjusted the cuffs on his crisp rose-pink shirt and tugged the material past the edge of his suit sleeves. Patrick slumped in his seat. He should be excited to be going out with Charles today.

Instead, he was mortified.

Curled up at Charles' away from the world, he had felt at

ease. But out here in the world, where people could see them together, he felt out of his depth and out of place.

He felt like they didn't fit so well together after all. He had thought this would be a casual adventure. Charles had explained, he needed to dress the part of a competing winery manager.

That requirement had resulted in too much contrast.

"What's wrong?" Charles asked.

Patrick fiddled with the switch that opened the window. "Nothing."

"Then what's with that look?"

"I'm just tired."

"I don't believe you. You slept like a baby."

"That whole saying is a myth. Babies don't sleep well at all. Ask any parent."

"Wow … okay."

"I was restless. Now I'm tired."

"You didn't move all night. You may have even drooled on my chest."

"So … what. I'm lying?"

Charles leaned forward in his seat. "What's gotten into you?"

"I don't want to do this." Patrick looked out the window. He needed to get out of there. He needed to get out of that damned abhorrent car. "Drop me off at home."

"But we've been planning this for days."

"I changed my mind." Patrick pounded on the privacy screen when he saw they were close to somewhere he could catch the bus home. The screen slid down. "Can we stop here, please?"

The driver nodded and pulled the car over to the side of the road.

"Are you planning on walking all the way home?" Charles asked.

"No, I'm bussing. Something you probably know nothing about."

"I bussed plenty when I was a kid."

Patrick flung the door open. "Well … adults do it too. Not all of us can afford a fancy car."

Charles moved to climb out after Patrick, but Patrick slammed the door shut behind him. Charles threw it open. "What the fuck, Patrick?"

"This was a mistake. It was all a mistake."

Charles climbed out of the car. "What's a mistake? Us?"

"Us. You … me … the whole bloody circus."

"Circus? What the hell are you talking about?"

"We shouldn't have done this. We should have stayed away from each other."

"Why? Because of Aubrey? I don't care about that anymore. This is about you and me."

"Exactly. It borders on perverse. What were we thinking?"

"We were thinking there was something special between us."

Patrick shook his head. "Doesn't matter. We shouldn't have done it."

Charles hobbled toward Patrick. "So … that's it? What happened to you being gentle with me? What happened to you not abandoning me … on the fucking roadside no less?"

Patrick stared at Charles, his breath heaving in his chest. He didn't want it to end like this, but he didn't know what else to do. They were universes apart. It would never work.

He tugged on the thick knot on his head. Even his damned hair didn't fit into Charles' world. Maybe he could cut his hair and change his clothes, but that wouldn't solve anything. He'd still be the guy from Rutland that Charles had picked up while slumming.

"We have nothing in common," Patrick said.

"Then how come we spent all week together proving otherwise?"

"We were fooling ourselves."

"You know that's not true."

"All of that doesn't matter." Patrick flung his arms to both sides. "Look at me. How can you stand to be seen with this?" Climbing out of limos. Walking into wineries. Charles with an unrefined monkey on his arm. The look on Charles' face wasn't one of agreement.

Charles closed in on Patrick and cupped Patrick's face in one hand. "Patrick … please." The look in Charles' eyes made Patrick reconsider everything he had just said. His heart was screaming at him to cease the destructive path he was on. His brain told him to take a few steps back.

He listened to his brain.

Charles ran his hands through his hair then reached for Patrick. There was anguish in Charles' eyes. "Patrick. I don't think you understand. I'm falling for you. I'm falling for the whole package."

Falling? What did he mean by that?

Love?

Charles couldn't be serious. They barely knew each other. This week had been epic … but falling in love? A warmth spread through Patrick's chest. Maybe Charles was telling the truth.

Patrick wandered back to where Charles was standing.

That would change everything. If Charles could look past everything he was lacking and be falling in love with him. His feelings were rapidly advancing in that direction.

"Say it again," Patrick said. "I need you to mean it."

"I'm falling for you, Patrick. Every fiber in me." Charles waved his hand for Patrick to approach the car. "Now, please, get back in the car. I'll take you wherever you want to go. My place—your place. The mall ... I don't fucking care. Just please get back in the car."

Patrick's resistance faded away. What they had *was* special. They'd gone from hating each other to depending on each other. They'd become devoted to each other.

Linked.

He needed to stop fighting it.

Charles held the door as Patrick climbed into the car. Once Patrick was settled, Charles slid into the seat across from him. "Where to?"

"It doesn't matter. Just take me somewhere I can be with you." Patrick reached forward and touched Charles' knee. "I can't do this alone. If I'm going to have an existential breakdown about you, I want you by my side. Ridiculous as that sounds."

"Nothing ridiculous about that."

Charles shifted seats to sit beside Patrick. He put his arm around Patrick and held him. "I've got you," Charles whispered. "You're safe with me." Patrick relaxed into his embrace.

Those were the words he needed to hear. Patrick's mind was in chaos. A rebellion of sorts. His heart wanted to storm his consciousness and conquer it. To quell it. Cause his brain to give up its objections. Relinquish itself to his emotions. It was giving him a headache.

"Can we go to my apartment? I want to grab those things to keep at your place."

"Really? Are you sure?"

"I have no idea. I'm just following my gut right now."

"All right." Charles hugged him tight against him.

It felt good—being held by Charles. He'd had a moment of panic but if he let his mind wander back to the last week, to the incredible connection they'd made, the turmoil subsided. Whether that meant he should bring belongings to Charles' was still being debated in his mind.

"I'm sorry," he said.

"It's all right. I get it." Charles kissed Patrick's head. "I've had moments of wondering what you see in me." He sighed. "Okay ... more than moments. The thoughts have dominated a lot of the time we've spent together this past week. I kept thinking you'd leave and never come back."

"And I almost did. I don't know why I did that."

"You're having the same problem as me. Believing you're not good enough."

"Fine pair." Patrick turned and gazed into Charles' eyes. "Can we agree that we are good enough for each other? I think that's a positive place to start."

Charles' chest heaved through a few breaths. He nodded but it wasn't with enthusiasm. It would still take some time for Charles to accept that truth about himself.

Patrick rapped on the privacy screen. "Can you pull in here?"

The car turned into a parking lot, blocking the driveway. He'd need to go further into the lot to find a space big enough to park. Mission Creek Greenway. It was packed.

"Let's go for a walk." Patrick threw open the door. "We can take it easy on your leg. I just need some fresh air." They crossed the pavilion to the entrance of the park.

Once on the trail, Patrick reached for Charles' hand. They walked hand-in-hand past other walkers and a few kids on bicycles. It was a crisp, beautiful sunny day.

The question had burned long enough.

"What did you mean by *falling for* ...?" Patrick asked.

"Let me start at the beginning."

Patrick squeezed Charles' hand. "A full story. I like that."

"It started at the wine event. Your company was unexpectedly pleasant. You fascinated me. I took notice of you." Charles smiled. "All of you. Even that damned bun. You weren't what I'd been imagining. You made an impression. You were more refined and knowledgeable about something I'm passionate about than I'd thought you'd be. It horrified me that I had enjoyed your company."

"Is that why you ran off to the washroom?"

"I needed a moment to clear my head." Charles squeezed Patrick's hand. "Later, on the boat, you were so carefree and uninhibited. It was what I needed after Aubrey spewed such vile things about both of us. And every time you looked away; I couldn't take my eyes off you.

"As we sat there, I realized I was attracted to you. When you stripped off your clothes on that beach ... damn. It did a number on my head because I hated you so much."

"We had that in common."

"In spades."

Charles brought their hands up to his lips and kissed Patrick's knuckles. "When you showed up in my hospital room, I didn't know what to make of that. I couldn't reconcile why you were there. Did you feel guilty about Aubrey cheating on me with you? Or were you just a nice guy?

"We had some great conversations. You were more than tolerable. You were there when I needed someone. Then you stumbled in drunk and told me why you liked me."

"That confused the hell out of you," Patrick said. "I could

see it in your eyes. That's why I stayed away."

Charles stopped walking. He turned to face Patrick. "I wish you hadn't. That nine weeks dragged on without you. Every day I waited for you to show up again."

"I had no idea."

Charles' brow dipped, sadness filling his face. "During those weeks, I realized the guy I had been hating might not be capable of lying. And I'd driven you off."

"I came back."

Charles smiled. "When I saw you standing at that door, a few puzzle pieces fell into place. I had hoped we might be friends. Except what I was feeling was so much more than friends. When you dropped me off at home, I was begging the universe for you to come inside and hold me."

"I would have if you'd asked me."

"In my heart, I knew that, but I was too scared to take that step with you."

"Then the very next day …"

"I attacked you at the winery. I don't know what came over me. Everything about you made sense. You weren't the vapid party boy. You weren't the prancing fucking pony. You were Patrick—and you were something I hadn't known I was missing in my life."

Patrick walked into Charles' outstretched arms and wrapped his arms around him.

"This past week," Charles continued. "You managed to draw feelings out of me that have never been part of my life. I've never felt so appreciated—and loved. I know that's a scary word, but that's what it feels like. There is so much love in the connection we've made."

Love.

It was there and it was beating strong.

A tear rolled down Patrick's cheek. "Dammit, Charles. You better kiss me."

The kiss filled his heart with reconciliation and commitment, and so many other things, he couldn't keep track. They were in this for the long haul.

Chapter Fourteen | Charles

For a moment there, Charles thought he had lost Patrick. It would have devastated him. He'd let his heart take every step forward it wanted to over the past week. Patrick had talked about allowing their relationship to grow organically and try not to limit it.

He had relaxed and followed Patrick's lead. What had developed between them was stunning. Finding time to connect when they were at work. Stolen kisses in his office. Then to go home with him. Laughing and teasing as they made dinner together. Working seamlessly. The ease of their evenings. And the sex … at times transcendent. Holding each other as they fell asleep. Morning showers together. Joking as they fought with the espresso maker. And back to work.

It was a routine he could see himself doing for the rest of his life.

They arrived at Patrick's apartment building and pulled off to one side. Patrick threw open the car door and leaned down to talk to Charles.

"Stay here. I'll only be a minute."

"Sure. Take your time."

After ten minutes passed, Charles wondered what was taking Patrick so long. He climbed out of the car and headed for the stairs Patrick had gone up. It took him longer than it would have if his leg wasn't bothering him. He walked down the passageway until he found an apartment with a door ajar. He could hear Patrick talking to himself inside. He pushed open the door.

Charles was immediately met by a stack of blue storage bins. He looked further into the apartment. The bins extended for the entire length of the hallway. He had to squeeze past them.

Once he was clear of them, he was met with a main living space stacked with more bins, at least fifteen of them, and piles of clothing, some with thrift store tags still on them, towers of magazines, mounds of stuffed animals, and wine bottles ... so many wine bottles. The bed was barely visible, half of it stacked with more stuffed animals and heaps of worn books.

A ripple of disbelief ran up his spine.

"Patrick? What the hell?"

Patrick popped out of the bathroom. "I told you to stay in the car."

"You were taking a long time." Charles wandered into the kitchen area. More wine bottles covered the stove along with empty boxes from microwavable food. In front of the cabinets, stacked plastic containers and bags upon bags of pop cans. A layer of cola boxes carpeted the floor.

"It's a bit messy," Patrick said as he moved a few things around from one pile to another.

"Patrick." Charles clapped his hand to his head. His heart was thundering. "This isn't just messy. This is a disaster area. How can you live like this?"

"You get used to it."

Charles' heart sank. His own life was so ordered and clean. This was too much.

"How, Patrick?"

Patrick touched Charles' arm. "I keep meaning to take things to the recycling depot. I just get busy." He looked around. "If all that was gone, it wouldn't be so bad."

Charles shook his head. "The clothes ... piles of them haven't even been worn. Even if you recycled the other stuff ... the bins ... what's even in them?"

Patrick peeled open the lid of one. "More clothes mostly. Some model boat kits."

"Model boats ... seriously. When was the last time you built one? I don't see any."

"I haven't gotten around to it yet, but they're there if I decide I want to do some."

"The stuffed animals?"

"How could I not? They have such cute little faces."

Charles took a step back from Patrick. He suddenly had no idea who Patrick was.

"Fuck, Patrick. This is insane. I had no idea." Charles stepped into the bathroom. The counter was completely covered in moisturizers, toners, shampoo, and conditioners.

His chest tightened. Patrick had never given him any indication he was like this. He was so neat and orderly at his house. Every instinct in him told him to run.

Charles turned and headed for the front door. "I can't do this. This is too much."

Patrick grabbed Charles' shoulder. "What do you mean you can't do this? Can't do us? Why? Because my place is a little disorganized?"

Charles spun back to face Patrick. "Disorganized? You're a hoarder, Patrick."

Patrick furrowed his brow. "It's not that bad."

"Yes ... yes, it is." Charles cupped Patrick's face and stroked his cheek. "I need to think about this. I have intense feelings for you, but I don't know if I can have this in my life."

Patrick grabbed Charles' hand. "I'll clean it up. I promise. I can get rid of everything."

Charles pulled away. "I need to go."

Patrick followed Charles into the passageway. "Please don't … I can fix this."

"I can't, Patrick … I just can't."

Walking away tore at his heart. Patrick had an addiction. One Charles was positive he couldn't live with. If they moved in together someday, it would eventually creep into their home.

He valued order too much.

Monday morning, Charles sat in his office staring at the computer screen. It was approaching Patrick's break time. Last week, Patrick had spent all his breaks in Charles' office.

Whispers of affection, kissing—a little groping.

The tears started again. All damned weekend, he'd been getting ugly on and off. He'd barely slept—the spot beside him in bed crushingly empty.

He'd been hiding in his office all morning. Dashing past the tasting room when he couldn't avoid leaving his safe space. He'd caught sight of Patrick. Captivating, adorable—loveable.

Charles was happy Patrick hadn't decided to pack in working for the winery. He really was an asset. But he was so much more than that.

He was in love with Patrick. Truly and fully sunk. He gripped his head. He was allowing all the affection he possessed to be eroded by Patrick's obsession to collect things. It seemed so minor when he thought back about it. How had that pulled them apart?

The turmoil in his head was making him crazy.

Someone knocked at his door.

He knew who it would be.

Patrick poked his head in. "Can we talk?"

It took a few moments for Charles to answer. He wasn't

sure.

"Come in. Close the door."

Patrick pressed the door closed behind him. He leaned against it. "I got rid of the wine bottles and pop cans yesterday. And I'm taking the magazines and cardboard for recycling tomorrow."

"That's barely going to make a dent."

Patrick smoothed his hair with one hand. "I'm trying. I've bagged up all the stuffed animals and I'm sorting through the clothes." He stepped forward and placed his hands on Charles' desk. "Not a single thing in that apartment is more important to me than us."

Patrick looked distraught. And it was obvious he hadn't slept much; dark rings blighted his beautiful brown eyes. It was possible he'd spent every waking hour trying to clean his apartment.

"When did it start?" Charles asked.

"I've always had a problem. My mom was a hoarder. I grew up in a cluttered house." Patrick rounded the desk to stand beside Charles. "Please … I'll give it all up. I promise."

Charles reached for Patrick's hand and clung to it. "I want to believe you. I do."

"What if I went to counseling?"

Charles took a deep breath. That was something he could get behind. Find help for Patrick. Ease the disease that had ruined everything for them.

"I'll pay for it," Charles said.

"But this is a deal breaker, isn't it?"

It hurt. It genuinely hurt his chest. His heart—his gut. He couldn't do it, though. Blow up his structured life—even for love.

"I can't, Patrick. I can't live like that."

Another rap on the door. It was Cindy this time.

"Aubrey is out here, Charles. He's insisting on seeing you."

Fuck. Now what?

Charles gave Patrick's hand a squeeze, released it, and rose to his feet. Patrick followed him through the door and down the hall to the tasting room. Aubrey was pacing back and forth.

"Finally!" Aubrey shouted. "Your staff were trying to tell me you weren't here."

Charles smirked. That was just like them. Trying to protect him.

"A misunderstanding. I'm here," he replied. "What do you want?"

"I've been thinking about us."

"I've already told you *no*."

"Come on, babe. We were good together, weren't we?"

Charles took a step back. "We were terrible together."

"Not all the time. We had good times. Lots of them."

Patrick wandered up behind Charles, then stood by his side.

"Oh, I see," Aubrey said and huffed out a laugh. "You've picked up the stray."

The color rose in Charles' cheeks. His anger was going to get the better of him in a minute. Aubrey needed to leave his winery. He needed to leave now.

"Get out of here!" Charles pointed toward the door.

Aubrey laughed. "That's rich. *You're* fucking the little boy toy now, are you?"

Charles clenched his fists. "He's not a toy." He looked around. His staff looked both confused and enlightened with confirmation. They had to have suspected something was happening between the two of them with Patrick spending every break in his office. But, they would have had no idea that Patrick had once been Aubrey's boyfriend.

Aubrey snorted a laugh. "Have you discovered his little secret yet? That should be enough to put you off. Mess up your prissy, perfect life."

A rush of emotion washed over Charles. Aubrey was wrong. Like a flash of clarity, Charles realized it didn't matter. The mess—the clutter—the hoarding. He was in love with Patrick no matter what. They could get through anything together. Aubrey wasn't going to sway him on this.

"I know about it," Charles said. "We're working on it."

"Working on it? Ha." Aubrey approached the counter. "He's chronic. Started bringing his shit into my townhouse, cluttering up the spare bedroom—the den, the garage. I was glad to get rid of him. He couldn't afford to move all his crap, so I took the whole lot of it to the dump."

Patrick stared at the floor.

Charles peered over at Patrick. "You amassed that much stuff in the short time you and Audrey have been apart? How did you afford it all?"

"Didn't," Patrick said. "Credit cards."

Great. The man he was in love with was a hoarder and he was in debt up to his eyeballs. His heart hammered in his chest. He wasn't going to give up on him.

He reached for Patrick's hand.

Patrick was quick to cling to it.

"As I said," Charles said. "We're working on it."

"Oh, for fuck's sake!" Aubrey nearly slammed his fist into a cabinet. "What we had was special, Charles. You're going to give all that up for a hoarding, slacker piece of trash?"

Charles' anger boiled. Aubrey had no idea what he'd thrown away. With Patrick—with him. "What we had was never special, Aubrey. What we had was abusive, destructive, and toxic. You tore me down." Charles dropped Patrick's hand and put his arm around him. "This man here ... he's done the opposite. He's built me up. Given me confidence. Made me realize my worth."

"He's lying to you. You'll never be able to do better than me."

"Why are you fighting so hard if I'm worthless." Charles looked at Patrick. "Because I'm with him?" He stared at Aubrey. "Does that make you jealous? Panicked that you let me go?"

Aubrey scowled at him. "I'm the only one who will ever love you—you'll always be mine. Patrick will dump you before the year is out. I guarantee it."

And there you had it. Aubrey's only motivation was possession. He needed to own him. Have Charles fall over himself trying to get things right. Make him feel like he was delusional all the time. Dismiss his feelings. Use him like an object.

Aubrey was the delusional one. Patrick had uncovered the truth in him. That he had value. That he was worthy. That he was desired for more than his looks. That he was cherished.

Every one of those things Patrick had brought to the forefront decided everything.

It needed to be said.

"I'm in love with Patrick. I'll do whatever it takes to be with him."

"Then you're a fool," Aubrey replied then spat on the floor. Once he stormed out through the doors, Charles released a heavy sigh. His body was vibrating. He felt on the edge of panic.

Aubrey had crawled beneath his boundaries.

"Let's go back to your office," Patrick said. "You need to get away from everything for a minute. Do some deep breathing. I'll stay with you. I'm not going anywhere."

Charles nodded. Patrick knew he had to escape from the world when he was feeling this overwhelmed. They'd spoken at length about it. His anxiety, his fears, and his struggle to present himself as a competent, strong leader every day. Aubrey had once again made him feel weak.

They rushed past the throng of employees that had gathered and headed for Charles' office. He sat on his sofa and Patrick joined him. Patrick leaned against Charles' shoulder. The closeness calmed him. Patrick turned, kissed Charles' cheek, and nuzzled against his neck.

"You're in love with me?" Patrick said.

Charles turned to face Patrick. "You know I am."

Patrick smiled, then furrowed his brow. "I'll go to counseling. I'll clean out my apartment. Get rid of everything. I promise. It'll never happen again."

"You don't have to get rid of everything. Let's just make it manageable."

"Just my favorite stuff."

Charles laughed. "I suspect that might be a lot. Can we pare it back more than that?"

"Ten bins?"

"Eight. We can keep them in the basement at home."

Patrick leaned back away from Charles. "Home? Are you asking me to move in with you?"

"I think I might be."

It had slipped from his mouth without thinking. Truthfully, he wanted to wake up with Patrick every morning and go to bed with him every night. Cook, appreciate wine—work, play and enjoy each other. Love—he wanted love. A few bins of stuff in the basement, he could handle. They'd have to work on keeping Patrick from accumulating more, but they could do that together.

"Let me finish cleaning my apartment before I move in. I want to prove to you; I can do it."

"You're going to make me wait to have you come home?"

"I need to do this—for us. You'll be fine." Patrick smiled. "I'll visit."

"Overnight visits?"

Patrick touched Charles' face. "That can be arranged."

Charles felt it in his heart, the intensity of the emotion in Patrick's eyes. They were bound together. They fit. They were devoted to one another. They were in this for the long haul

Chapter Fifteen | Patrick

Patrick plopped himself down on his bed and looked around his apartment. He was winning. It was slow—but he was winning. The kitchen was cleaned out. It had been nice to use the stovetop last night. The jars, yogurt containers, and empty meal boxes that had been littering the small kitchenette were gone. In the bed-sit area, it had been gut-wrenching, but he'd let all but ten stuffed animals go. The clothes presented more of a challenge. There was so much promise in each garment. Especially now. He wanted to look presentable around Charles. He divided them into piles. Pants, shirts, coats, and shoes. Four of his bins had contained shoes and nothing else.

When he saw how high each pile was, he broke down and wept. He wasn't sure how it had gone so wrong. It was going to take weeks to slowly dole out his extra clothing to the thrift stores in town without overloading them. It had been weeks already since Charles had invited him to move in with him. Working such long hours at the winery meant Patrick hadn't been able to dedicate as much time as he'd like to clear out his apartment.

Charles was coming over today to help.

Patrick waded through a pile of empty bins and answered the door. Charles was wearing blue jeans and a black t-shirt. It made Patrick smile. Charles was prepared to put in some work. He rarely saw Charles dressed this casually. Aside from when they were alone together.

"Hey, hon." Charles moved in for a kiss. As always, it

almost brought Patrick to his knees. Now that he knew Charles loved him, the affection between them held so much more meaning.

Patrick wrapped his arms around Charles and hugged him.

"Thank you for doing this—helping me."

"You sounded a bit defeated on the phone."

"I'm having trouble with my clothes. I have no idea what to get rid of."

Charles surveyed the piles. "Take it in stages, I think. Go through each piece." He picked up a pair of pants and looked at the label. "Some of these are worth keeping."

"I'll grab an empty bin for the thrift store donations. I'm going to close my eyes and let you work on the pants. I'll try to slog my way through the shirts."

"Sounds like a plan."

Patrick kept himself from peeking at what Charles was doing. Charles had good taste. Patrick trusted him to make acceptable decisions. He was a bit startled to see the lean resulting pile. The thrift store bin was overflowing, and Charles had grabbed a second and third one.

Charles touched the pile of pants he had deemed acceptable. "I'll take these back to the house. Wash them. And hang them in our closet."

Patrick grinned. "*Our* closet, hey."

"Soon." Charles licked his lips. "God, you're sexy when you're thinking about us."

"Then, I'm almost always sexy."

Charles wrapped Patrick up in his arms. "I would agree with that statement." He looked down at the messy piles of shirts on the bed. "How's it going over here?"

"Slower than you." Patrick had two evenly sized piles. Both with too many shirts in them. He pointed at one pile. "These can definitely go." He placed his hand on the other pile. "I need help with these. Can you go through them? I'll start on the shoes."

Charles touched Patrick's face. "I love that you trust me.

"I love that you love me."

Charles descended on his mouth. Patrick hadn't worked up to saying it aloud yet. But he did—he loved Charles. He was scared to have the words spill out from between his lips. Scared that if he said it, everything would evaporate. Jump too soon— and have Charles back out.

Three hours later and they were struggling with six full bins and five bags of clothing, headed for the door and down the stairs. Charles had rented a cargo van for the month. He agreed to pepper the items throughout the city's thrift stores over the next two weeks.

They'd spent a few minutes sorting through Patrick's bathroom. Patrick was to pick out one of each product. It was his homework. Finish that then he could head over to Charles'.

Patrick watched Charles drive away without him.

With the extra motivation, the choice of products became worthless. His life with Charles was more important than any damned deodorant. He finished clearing his bathroom, took a black garbage bag out to the dumpster, chucked it in, and leaped into his truck.

Charles was grilling some steaks for dinner tonight. Patrick wouldn't be staying the night. He needed to start organizing more of his belongings early in the morning. He'd left the hardest task for last. Sorting through the model boat kits. He'd always seen himself as a boat person. Ever since he was a kid. His grandfather had built model boats. He imagined creating a tradition. A love of boats. Something he would pass down to his kids if he had them.

When he had them.

He was struggling to believe it might someday be an actual option for him. Neither of them had spoken about having children in their lives someday. It was too soon. Too soon to assume that this relationship would go that far. They'd only been together a little over two months.

He watched the flash-flash-flash of the streetlights as he drove past them in the dark. How had love come into play so early? Their emotions for each other had started strong—with hatred. It seemed the road from hatred to love hadn't been as far as one might think.

They'd already been on each other's minds for a very long time. They weren't new to one another. Discovering they had an attraction. Letting their guard down and finding out that neither one of them was a monster; they had pursued where their emotions might carry them.

Love.

It had just happened.

That first week together had been the clincher. Spending day and night in each other's company had been like ten dates all rolled into an extended one.

You could fall in love in ten dates.

Patrick breathed in and steadied his thoughts. It was more than that. More than an extended date. It felt as if they'd been destined to connect. That all they had been put through, being psychologically abused by Aubrey, had led them to one day finding each other.

He pulled into Charles' driveway. Someday soon, this would be him coming home. Coming home to the man he loved. He knocked and walked into the front entry. Charles was arguing with someone on the phone. The smell of burning steaks permeated the air.

"That's ludicrous," Charles shouted into the phone. "She can't just come back now and start demanding stuff like that." Silence while he listened. "Then she'll see me in court."

Charles slammed his phone down on the counter.

"What's going on?" Patrick stroked Charles' arm and gently gripped his wrist.

"My mother has decided to make an appearance. She found out my father died. Thinks she deserves everything he left me."

"Were they still married?" Patrick knew a little bit about estates and wills. His mom had been executor when her parents died years apart. She'd shared everything she was going through.

"God only knows."

"Makes a difference."

"My lawyer is looking into it." Charles pushed past Patrick. "Made me burn the damned steaks. I've got two more in the fridge. Can you grab them?"

Patrick retrieved the butcher-paper-wrapped package and headed for the patio. Charles was disposing of two blackened hunks of meat onto a plate. Patrick unwrapped the package as Charles shut off the flames and took a wire brush to the grill. Patrick pressed his lips together, stifling a grin as Charles scrubbed and grunted, mumbling, and swearing beneath his breath. When Charles was done, he took a deep breath. "Okay, let's start this again." He fired up the barbeque.

"Want to talk about your mother?"

"Nope."

Patrick wrapped his arms around Charles' waist as Charles threw the two steaks onto the grill. "Can I get you a glass of wine?"

"Now you're heading in the right direction."

Patrick wandered into the kitchen, retrieved two glasses,

and lifted the open bottle sitting on the counter. Châteauneuf-du-Pape. A French red. Perfect for steak. He peered into the oven. Charles was roasting an assortment of root vegetables and fresh herbs. They smelled amazing.

"Everything to your satisfaction?" Charles swept Patrick up in his arms.

"Always."

Patrick melted into Charles' kiss. He didn't object when Charles pulled on the elastic keeping his hair in a knot. After a few tugs, Patrick's thick strands of hair landed on his shoulders.

Charles preferred it that way—down. When they were at home.

Their home.

"That's better." Charles leaned back and perused every visible inch of him. Patrick smiled and touched Charles' lips. Charles made a game of sucking Patrick's finger into his mouth.

He would let Charles eat him right there in the kitchen.

Except.

"The steaks are overcooking," Patrick reminded Charles.

Charles groaned and released him. "As soon as we're done … I want dessert."

"With whipped cream?"

Charles stopped his retreat to the patio and turned around. "Oh, now you've done it. You've ruined my entire appetite for these steaks."

"No dessert without eating your dinner." Patrick removed his coat, tossed it on one of the bar stools lining the counter, and poured two glasses of wine.

"So brutal." Charles stepped onto the patio. He fussed about for a few minutes then shut off the gas. The steaks were bordering on medium-rare on one side, but the other side was rare and gorgeous. They talked about the winery while they ate. They'd be gearing up for harvesting grapes for ice wine soon. The temperatures had been dropping overnight.

Patrick was looking forward to the long nights ahead out in the vineyards. It was all hands on deck when it came to ice wine. Time was of the essence. Even Charles would join in. Patrick would get to see how those callouses on Charles' hands had been formed. Charles had told Patrick about his childhood and teenage years, growing up around his father's winery.

The good times and bad.

His father had stopped short of beating Charles, but not by much.

"You'll love it," Charles said. "The crisp, cold air biting at your skin. Filling your lungs. Your fingers going numb the longer you work."

"Why is that part fun?"

"It's like a badge of honor, fumbling for grapes out in the vineyard in the dark and cold. You conquer the entire experience with your team. It bonds you."

"Sounds romantic."

"It will be with you by my side."

"I'm looking forward to it."

Charles rose to his feet. "I'm looking forward to dessert. Did you eat everything?"

"I'm a good boy. I cleaned my plate."

Charles smiled. "All right, then. Good boys get to play in the hot tub."

Patrick hummed in appreciation of the idea. They had made love in every room of that house, but the hot tub was one of his favorites. It felt risqué being outside. Like the neighbors might overhear them. The idea thrilled him. He couldn't move fast enough. He headed for the stairs to the lower level. Charles' leg had healed enough that stairs weren't an issue anymore.

He stripped off his clothes in the family room and opened the sliding door to outside. The gust of cold January air started him shivering. Charles was right behind him. They made a dash for the snow-covered patio, removed the hot tub cover, and slipped into the steaming hot water.

Patrick drifted to where Charles was seated and straddled his lap. He tipped his head back and wet his hair. Charles was staring at Patrick when he straightened up.

"God, you're beautiful," Charles said then kissed him; slow and tender. Patrick felt it right through to the tips of his toes. So much love. Charles moved his hand through the water and took a hold of Patrick's cock. His touch was gentle—unassuming.

Patrick sighed as Charles stroked it.

He knew Charles' hard cock would be bobbing between them. He took Charles' thick shaft in one hand and slipped his palm up and down its length. They pressed their foreheads together. Their hot breath united in the cold air. Heaving puffs. Patrick released Charles' cock and shifted further up in his lap. Charles wrapped his arms around Patrick and clung to his back.

"What are you doing?" he asked.

"I think it's time." Patrick ground his ass against Charles' cock.

"Are you sure?"

Of course, he was sure. He loved the man with his entire soul. He wanted to feel him—unsheathed. "We've both been tested. Negative."

Charles' chest rose and fell. "You have no idea how much I want this."

"I'm pretty sure I do."

Charles pulled Patrick tighter to him, then slipped his hands onto Patrick's ass. He assisted in lifting Patrick and lowering him onto his cock. Patrick's hands were between them, guiding him.

Patrick rolled his head back and stared up at the sky as Charles slid firmly inside.

He closed his eyes and clung to Charles' shoulders.

Fucking glorious.

The rock of Charles' hips was serene and loving as Patrick kept himself afloat just above Charles' hips. He gripped the edge of the hot tub and shifted onto his knees. He lifted and descended fully on Charles' cock. Charles leaned forward and brushed his hand across Patrick's hair. "I fucking adore you," he whispered in Patrick's ear.

"Show me," Patrick whispered back. He wrapped his hands around the back of Charles' neck as Charles kissed him. He clutched handfuls of Charles' hair as Charles deepened the kiss.

Charles pulled away and gazed into Patrick's eyes.

"You've changed me," he said.

Patrick touched Charles' cheek. "How so?" The eyes staring at him were so intense; profound love flowed from them. Love and absolute adoration. It was breathtaking.

"You've unlocked something I didn't know was there."

"Self-worth?"

Charles blinked. "It feels deeper than that."

"Self-love?"

Patrick could sense the gears in Charles' mind grinding through the possibility that he loved himself. It was beautiful to watch. The windows opening. The light coming in.

He stroked Charles' face then ran his thumb across Charles'

bottom lip.

"There he is," Patrick said. "There's the man I've fallen in love with."

He could finally say it aloud. There were few things he could keep contained. This had been different. Love. He had needed to be sure Charles wasn't going to back out. That Charles' insecurities weren't going to pull them apart. That he wouldn't end up heartbroken.

Patrick hadn't thought Charles' facial expression could radiate more love. But there it was. Patrick's words of love had unlocked yet another level in Charles' heart.

Tears spilled and streaked down Charles' cheeks.

"Patrick ... I'm absolutely desperate for you."

Patrick kissed him and rocked his hips. Charles' cock retreated and thrust. He wanted one thing from this incredible man tonight. To be truly joined. Patrick increased his pace, sliding up and down. Rocking—grinding. He dug his fingernails into Charles' shoulders as he crested into the water. Charles wasn't far behind. Patrick liked to think he felt himself being filled.

He cupped Charles' face in both hands as he came to rest in Charles' lap.

"I love you," he whispered.

Charles smiled. "I love you too."

The words had finally been shared. A true expression of the devotion that had been there for a long time. Now both their hearts were on the line. Jointly: miraculous—and terrifying.

Patrick captured Charles' mouth.

They were in this together.

Chapter Sixteen | Charles

Charles rolled over onto his side. Patrick was sound asleep beside him. They hadn't intended to make this an overnight visit but the shared words of love and decision to ditch the condoms had led to an evening of lovemaking. It had been early in the morning when they'd finally slept.

He lay there and watched Patrick. They'd taken a huge step last night. Expressing their love for one another. Charles stroked a strand of Patrick's hair. He would give up anything for this man.

The thought of losing Patrick brought a moment of panic. He had to breathe through it.

Stop—just stop.

Patrick wasn't going anywhere.

He had to keep reminding himself. Patrick had told him he loved him last night. That had taken a lot of courage. He knew Patrick was cautious about admitting his love. To speak it aloud. To take the risk that exposing his feelings might bring on a problem that tore them apart.

Like him, Patrick had experienced bad luck with men.

Now they were truly together. Despite their differences. They were opposites in every sense of the word. But that's what made them special. Their differences fit together.

Patrick mumbled something in his sleep. Charles couldn't make it out other than his name. He pulled the covers over his shoulder. Patrick was dreaming about him.

The thought lulled him back to sleep.

A few hours later, the sun streamed through the windows. Someone had thrown open the room-darkening curtains. The smell of coffee and bacon drifted up the stairs. Charles rolled onto his back. This was how he liked to wake up. The start of a perfect day with all its possibilities.

"Breakfast!" Patrick shouted from downstairs in the kitchen.

Charles groaned. He was so glad it was Sunday, and they had the day off work. There would be a lot of napping happening today. Napping and making love. They had the whole day to enjoy each other. No responsibilities. No distractions.

Except.

My mother.

He furrowed his brow. There was no way he was letting her ruin his day. His lawyer had said he'd call again on Monday regarding her claim. Let him know what he'd found out about the status of his parents' marriage. It was hard to believe they hadn't proceeded with a divorce.

It had gone so wrong for his parents. From love to animosity. The opposite direction he and Patrick had traveled. Who knew what was in their future? All he knew was marriage was supposed to be a sacred institution. Something you didn't enter into lightly. You needed to be sure.

He sat up and looked at the empty spot beside him. He was sure he never wanted that spot in his bed to be empty ever again in his life. Was Patrick the man to fill that role, though?

Charles had a lot to think about.

He rose and threw on a silk kimono. He left it open. It would an easy-access kind of day. No need to put clothes on. Patrick hummed with appreciation as Charles entered the kitchen.

"Yum," Patrick said as he closed in on Charles. He stroked his hand along Charles' bare cock. It was already on the way to being primed. "Breakfast first. I don't want the bacon to get cold."

Charles groaned. Patrick was entirely naked except for an apron, and he had made bacon, eggs, and pancakes. He was obviously expecting them to need some energy. He looked around the kitchen. Patrick had been cleaning as he cooked. He turned his gaze to the table.

He spotted the maple syrup.

He grinned and formulated a few plans for that sticky syrup as soon as they finished eating. It was more mouth-watering than the spread before him; Patrick covered in the taste of boiled maple sap. He took a seat and set in, devouring everything Patrick kept piling on his plate.

Once they were finished eating, he lifted the syrup from the table and rose to his feet. He wasn't even interested in drinking the rest of his coffee. An oddity for him.

"What on earth do you have planned for that?" Patrick smirked, removed the apron, let it fall to the floor, and hoisted himself onto the edge of the kitchen counter.

"Lie down." Charles popped open the top of the syrup bottle and ran his thumb across the rim, then stuck his finger in his mouth. Patrick arranged his body on the marble surface.

"Lift your arms," Charles said and Patrick obeyed.

Charles lifted the bottle and tipped it. The sweet syrup drooled through the hairs under Patrick's arms. Then across his collarbone to the other underarm. Down and across each nipple. Along the center of his body. Patrick squirmed and undulated his hips. His cock was firm and gorgeous, anxious to be devoured. Charles poured syrup down its length, then coated his balls.

He set the bottle down. He was going to start from the top.

The shower was hot and steamy. For more than one reason. Patrick was currently on his knees bringing him a scorching amount of pleasure.

The syrup had proven itself to be a sticky adversary. Charles' hands, face, and hair had ended up covered in it. And they'd practically needed a scrub brush to wash it from Patrick's skin.

Charles placed his hands on Patrick's head and held him steady. He rocked his hips, plunging his cock into the warm depth. He grunted. There it was. Right there.

Patrick gripped Charles' thighs, dug his fingers in, and clung to Charles as he spilled down Patrick's throat. After a few shudders from Charles, Patrick rose to his feet and kissed Charles. Patrick's mouth was wet and musky. His lips; plump and warm.

Charles wrapped his arms around the man he loved more than life itself.

"Let's do your hair again," he whispered to Patrick.

"Good idea." Patrick ran his fingers through the hair at the base of his neck. "It feels like it's still clumped together." He reached for the shampoo and handed it to Charles.

Charles poured a generous amount of organic rosemary-mint shampoo into his hand, then started on Patrick's hair. He loved washing it. He'd taken over doing it during their showers. He felt like he was paying homage to Patrick. He had so much respect for his partner.

He hummed to himself.

Partner.

They had moved to that place in their relationship. They were committed to each other. They were moving forward together. In love. Side-by-side. Hand-in-hand.

He kissed the sensitive spot at the base of Patrick's neck, disregarding the taste of the shampoo. He let his lips linger there. He placed his hands on Patrick's shoulders.

"I love you so much," Charles said.

Patrick turned and wrapped his arms around Charles.

"I love you too."

It was coming easier to them. The words of love. For him, it started in his gut, filled his chest, rose through his throat, and spilled from his lips; the sincerity like nothing he'd ever spoken before.

The doorbell rang and broke the moment.

The best Charles could do was to quickly towel off and put his kimono back on, skin still damp, hair a wet mess. He was expecting a delivery.

He opened the door to a face he thought he would never see again.

"Mother."

"Charles." She frowned. "Did I catch you at a bad time?"

Charles almost laughed aloud. He hadn't seen her in over twenty-five years, and she was worried because she had caught him in the shower. He wasn't sure what to do next.

His lifetime of proper manners took over.

"Come in." Charles stepped back and fully opened the door. His mother walked into the front entry as Patrick made his way down the stairs in a fluffy white bathrobe.

Charles looked over his shoulder at him.

"Mother, this is Patrick. My boyfriend—my partner."

There was a slight twitch and a furrowed brow from his mother. She would have had no idea he was gay. And he sure as hell wasn't going to hide it.

His mother undid the top two buttons of her coat. Charles

stepped toward her and helped her remove the thick, woolen garment. He wandered over to the closet and hung it up.

Charles was very conscious of the fact he was naked beneath his kimono. And so was Patrick beneath the bathrobe. When Charles took a seat, he tugged at the thin fabric to completely cover himself. Patrick decided to stand behind the sofa.

"What brings you to my door when you haven't bothered for twenty-six years."

Jumping right in.

"I heard your father died."

"Yes, my lawyer told me you were in town sniffing around."

His mother fussed with her skirt, then sat in one of the leather armchairs.

"I was hoping we could settle this between us," she said.

"Settle what? You left."

She looked around the room. "You've done well."

"I've worked hard for it."

"Your father left you the winery. It seems like someone else has taken it over. I went there looking for you. The manager said you were the general manager somewhere else."

"I sold it. I wanted nothing more to do with the place."

"Your father would be heartbroken."

Charles rose to his feet. "My father disowned me." He turned and pointed at Patrick. "He didn't like the idea that I only wanted to find love with men." He turned back to his mother. "I inherited the winery because I was his son, regardless of what he thought of me. Not you—me."

"You didn't deserve it. Your father and I built that winery together. Twelve years of struggling and trying to make ends meet. That means something. I'm owed something."

"I worked that winery for fourteen years. My hard work meant something too." Charles crossed his arms. "How much to make you go away?"

"That winery was worth millions."

Charles laughed. "You're not getting millions out of me."

His mother scowled at Charles. "I want enough to buy a house."

"That's a rather broad number." Charles headed for his office. He came back with his checkbook. He sat on the sofa, pen at the ready. "Four-fifty. That's all I'm doing." He looked up at her. "And you're not getting this today. It'll be going through my lawyer. You'll have some papers to sign saying you'll leave me alone from now on." He filled out a couple of fields but didn't sign the check. He lay the pen down on the coffee table. "That's all you're getting."

His mother nodded. "That'll do." She rose from her chair. "Thank you, Charles."

Charles huffed out a laugh. "Great doing business with you." He followed her to the front entry, retrieved her coat, and ushered her out the front door. He pressed the door shut.

He shuddered through a guttural moan.

Then the fallout happened.

Charles collapsed to the ground, sobbing. It had struck him like a lightning bolt, the anguish. Patrick rushed to his side, kneeled beside him, and put his arm around Charles' shoulders.

"I'm here." Patrick stroked Charles' head and massaged his neck. "Come on." He encouraged Charles to stand. "Let's sit down." He directed him back to the living room.

For the next thirty minutes, the sofa was the safe space where Charles could cry and lament. Patrick continued to hold Charles as he rolled through torrents of emotions. He was devasted by the coldness of the interaction. He was glad it was over. He was feeling justified by his long-standing opinion of his mother being true. He was grateful his mother hadn't connected with him before Patrick came into his life. She'd rattled him but she hadn't broken him.

Not once had he felt like it was his fault. That she had stayed away because he was no good. Her actions were all on her. Her decision to abandon him had nothing to do with his worth.

Patrick had helped him reveal that to himself.

"You feel better?" Patrick rubbed Charles' back. Charles had stopped crying. He inhaled and released a long sigh. The potential of grief had been a long time coming but now he was free of it.

Charles turned and gazed into Patrick's eyes.

"You're the most amazing person I've ever had in my life."

"I feel the same."

An uncomfortable clenching sensation rolled through Charles' gut.

He needed to be somewhere else but here. A new surrounding. A new place to express his love for Patrick. He needed to get out of town.

"Let's get away for a few days," he said. "We have some time before the ice wine harvest."

Patrick tipped his head. "Where?"

He knew exactly where.

"To one of the most romantic cities in Canada." Charles kissed Patrick. "I want to show you Victoria. I think you'll fall in love with the ocean."

"I'm already in love with you. But I'm willing to expand on that."

"How about tomorrow? You and me. I'll book a flight."

A slightly worried look flitted across Patrick's face. "I've never been anywhere before."

Charles' eyebrows rose. "You've never been on a plane?"

Patrick shook his head.

Charles kissed Patrick. "You'll be fine." He touched Patrick's face. "I have so many amazing places to show you. We can spend the rest of our lives traveling around the globe together."

Oh, my god.

That had slipped out. *The rest of our lives*. His heart tripped around in his chest. Maybe he'd spoken too soon. They were still new. They hadn't talked about future plans with each other. What they wanted. Where they saw their relationship heading. Charles held his breath.

Patrick kissed his forehead. "I'd love that."

A rush of relief and exhilaration flooded Charles' body. Patrick was thinking long-term. This incredible man saw them living a life together. He leaped to his feet and went looking for his phone. Plans needed to be made. This would be a trip Patrick would never forget.

Chapter Seventeen | Patrick

The words Charles had spoken had caught Patrick by surprise. *The rest of our lives*. He fussed with his bathrobe while Charles headed for the bedroom to look for his phone. He leaned back and stared at the ceiling. His own words had tripped out of his mouth. *I'd love that*.

Had he meant it? He wasn't sure. It was a huge step to talk about forever together. He wasn't sure they were there. He hadn't even moved in with Charles yet.

"Booked the flight and the hotel." Charles approached the sofa. He lifted his gaze from his phone and looked at Patrick. He scowled. "What's wrong?"

Patrick leaned forward and placed his elbows on his knees. He looked up at Charles. "We both just agreed to *forever*. Is that where we are?"

Charles sat down. "That's where I'd like to be. That's what my heart is telling me."

His own heart was telling him the same thing. But he didn't necessarily trust his heart. It had led him astray before. He studied Charles' expression. So much hope and apprehension.

Follow your heart.

Patrick cupped Charles' face. "Then I'm right there with you."

He could see Charles' breath had been faltering in his chest. He'd scared the heck out of Charles by delaying his answer. He needed to make that right.

"Make love to me. True love. Show me a love that will last

forever."

Charles moved toward Patrick and pressed him over on the sofa. He stretched out as Charles closed in against him; his magnificent lover hovering above him.

"You are my forever love," Charles said.

"And you're mine."

Charles descended and took Patrick's mouth. It was a kiss like none other they had ever shared before. They were sealing a pact. A promise to one another.

An entire life together.

The flight hadn't freaked Patrick out as much as he thought it would. During the take-off and landing, he had gripped Charles' hand. It was all he had needed to settle his nerves.

They gathered their luggage at the carousel and headed for the door. He wasn't sure what to expect. Charles had told him it was warmer on the coast than the interior.

The scent of salt air immediately hit his senses. Charles took a deep breath of it beside him. Patrick shifted his luggage into his other hand. He wasn't sure he liked the smell.

"I love being on the island," Charles said.

Patrick looked around once they were outside the airport. In the distance, he could see lush greenery. There were no other buildings in sight. "Is this it?"

"No." Charles stepped out and hailed a cab. "We're in Sidney. It'll take us another thirty minutes to get where we're going. Depending on the traffic."

Patrick tossed his luggage in the cab's trunk beside Charles'. They climbed into the backseat. The drive took half as long as the flight. That still blew Patrick's mind. That fifty minutes in the air had carried them from the interior to the island that housed their provincial parliament.

He peered out the window as they approached downtown. It was so much bigger than Kelowna. Street after street of busy streets. Pedestrians, tall buildings, and traffic. Patrick gripped the handrest on the door as they approached the hotel Charles had been going on about.

It was situated across from the Inner Harbour and looked like a massive castle. Patrick had looked up its history on his phone. He loved knowing the stories behind structures.

The architect Francis Rattenbury was hired to construct the hotel. It opened in 1908. He also designed the parliament buildings and a bank in the downtown core. In 1935, he was murdered. Accused of his murder, his second wife and her lover, an 18-year-old gardener. The wife was acquitted, her lover sentenced to hang. Distressed by the verdict, the wife took her life just days after the verdict was read. Then one final twist. The lover's sentence was lessened to a life term, and he was released to serve in the Second World War. He later married and passed away in 2000.

It was a tale similar to the ones he would tell tourists back home. Patrick breathed out a sigh. Back when he still worked on the tour boats. His life had changed so much.

He had finished his wine courses.

He was in love.

Patrick followed Charles into the immense foyer. A burgundy antique-looking rug covered most of the floor space in the entry. Tall white columns. An upper balcony. And a cap of sorts above the upper floor; all windows. The sun poured into the space.

It was breathtaking.

They slipped into the elevator with the bellhop. Stepping out of it, they were greeted by an elegant corridor. They passed a seating area. An antique console flanked by two upholstered chairs. Above the console, a picture of a woman in 1800s garb. It almost felt a little creepy.

Their room was like something out of a magazine. They entered the living room space. A sofa—two armchairs. Straight ahead an electric coal fireplace. To the left a full dining room.

Charles headed in the opposite direction from the dining room toward an open door. Inside was a king-sized bed with crisp white bedding. Patrick pulled his luggage up to the side of the bed and wandered into the bathroom attached to the bedroom. Two full cream-colored cabinets with a sink each. He turned. Behind him a massive white claw-foot tub.

He touched the porcelain. They'd definitely be taking a dip in that later.

Patrick took a deep breath.

It was bigger than most apartments he'd ever been in. He headed back to the bedroom, flopped down on the bed, and stared up at the elegant tray ceiling.

Between the extravagance of the suite and the check Charles had begun to write for his mother, it suddenly occurred to him that his boyfriend might be loaded.

"What's going to happen with your mom and the money?"

Charles heaved out a sigh. "Most of my money is locked up in investments. I'll need to speak to my financial advisor. Figure out the best way to put my hands on that kind of money."

"But you have it … that kind of money?"

Charles sat on the bed beside Patrick. "Does that bother you?"

"Bother me?" Patrick sat up and leaned his head against Charles' shoulder. "No. There's just so much I still don't about you. There's so much you don't about me."

Charles entwined his fingers with Patrick's and held his

hand.

"Tell me a secret about you," he said. "Something you haven't told anyone else."

Patrick smirked. "Where to start." He tapped his lips. "I once stole an expensive pair of sunglasses from a department store."

"Really?"

Patrick snorted. "I was five. My mom made me march right back in there and return them."

"That's not a secret if your mom knew."

"Okay." Patrick paused. He hadn't told anyone about this. "I was a teenager. I was working in a fast-food restaurant. There was this guy from school—a football player. At school, he ignored me. While we were working, he'd tease me. I thought he was interested.

"One day, I went into the back room for cups, and he followed me. He was all over me—kissing me—touching me. He convinced me to drop my pants and stroke my cock."

Charles kissed Patrick's cheek. "You don't have to tell me the rest. I think I can guess."

Patrick furrowed his brow. "The picture he took circulated through the whole school."

"Fuck, Patrick. I'm sorry."

"Not really a secret, but it's not something I share with anyone in my adult life. You're the first person I've ever told." Patrick sighed. "Everyone at school knew I was gay after that."

"I didn't come out until my late twenties. Mostly because I was afraid of my dad. Had plenty of male lovers in university. In secret. Started to hate living a lie. I wanted my freedom."

Patrick smiled. "And now you have it."

Charles hugged Patrick to him.

"I hate that you went through all that ridicule at school."

"Turned out not so bad." Patrick shrugged. "Made some great friends I wouldn't have if I hadn't been outed. I'm still friends with a lot of them." He rose to his feet. "Does this fancy hotel have a restaurant where I can get a great big, fat burger? I'm starving."

"No, but I know where does."

They left through the foyer and turned right toward downtown. The street, Government, they took was quaint with all sorts of shops. Books, chocolates, indigenous clothes and art, cigars, Irish linens—kilts. And an assortment of tourist trap shops, offering all sorts of items with Victoria emblazoned on them. They peered around inside a couple of shops. Decided to return to a tea shop the next day for tea and dessert. They arrived at the pub they'd been heading for.

The burger was fabulous. And the music was entertaining. An Irish band was playing, and people were singing along and dancing. It was a fantastic atmosphere. So different from anything available in Kelowna, even on a weekend. Charles told him that live music was big in Victoria, and if Patrick wanted, they could visit a few different places to check it out.

They decided that was a good plan and spent the rest of the night hopping from venue to venue and dancing until they were exhausted. They finally crawled back to the hotel at 2 am.

They were too tired to make love. They both passed out until the sun rose and shone through the thin white curtains. They hadn't thought to close the thicker, embroidered ones.

"I don't want to get up," Charles said.

Patrick propped himself on one arm, smiled, and walked his fingers up Charles' chest. He stopped at Charles' chin and touched his bottom lip. "We could stay in bed for the morning."

"I need to make a trip to the washroom first."

"Me too. I brought supplies. I desperately need to feel you

inside me."

Charles pulled Patrick down for a kiss.

"Absolutely," he whispered against Patrick's lips.

Patrick flipped the covers back. "Go on." He pushed Charles' shoulder. "Scoot." Charles walked to the bathroom. Patrick couldn't contain himself. He whistled at the perfect ass crossing the floor. Charles looked back at him, snorted and smirked, and disappeared into the bathroom.

He spread out in bed. Arms and legs—starfish style. He grinned at absolutely nothing, He'd never been so happy. Charles was perfect. Their life together was perfect. When they got home, he was going to make the final push and finish cleaning out his apartment. He'd already given notice for the end of the month. Another fourteen days left. He was sure he could do it.

Charles wandered to the end of bed wearing Patrick's favorite outfit—nothing. He truly was a beautiful man. Head to toe. His only flaw was the scar that ran the length of his outer thigh, and one small sliver of missing eyebrow with a white line. The remnants from the car accident.

"What are you thinking about?" Charles asked. "You look deep in thought."

"You—and that damned apartment. I want to move in with you before the end of the month."

"What needs done still?"

"Cleaning mostly. All that stuff created a bit of a mess."

"Do you want me to hire cleaners to come in?"

Patrick shook his head. "No. I want to do this. It's my fault. I need to fix it."

"Can I help, at least?"

He wasn't sure. Charles was no stranger to hard work even if he hadn't done much for many years. Patrick reached for

Charles and held his hand. It would be nice to have some company.

"I'd like that."

"Good—settled." Charles climbed onto the bed. "Off with you. Bathroom."

It was past noon before they emerged from their hotel room.

They started the afternoon with a bit of decadence and had high tea in the hotel. After that, they went for a stroll along the Inner Harbour to walk off the number of calories in pastries, scones, clotted cream, and jams they had ingested. It had made for a filling late breakfast.

They mounted some steps and took a few pictures of each other in front of the parliament building's fountain. They stopped short of doing a tour. Even Patrick wasn't that interested.

Politics weren't high on his interest list.

"Do you want to go to fisherman's wharf?" Charles asked.

"What's there?"

"Restaurants …"

"God, I couldn't eat another bite."

"There are also some cool floating homes down there."

Patrick linked arms with Charles. "It's a beautiful day. I'm up for it." They walked the seawall past a few boat docks and expensive apartments overlooking the water. Charles pointed out a sea lion. It was just a tiny face breaking the water for a breath and to look around.

Patrick was fascinated by the inlet. Small passenger ferries raced back and forth in the water. Charles suggested they take one back downtown after. As they came around a bend, a seaplane took off from the water. It was so busy. It reminded

Patrick of a book he used to read as a child. Where you had to spot all the activities and occupations of the characters on the book's pages.

Next, up a slight incline and down a road, they were at the top of a marina. They made their way down the ramp. Charles was right. Colorful floating homes lined a couple of docks. Most of the main dock was covered with restaurants and eating areas.

The air was filled with the smell of fish and chips.

And seagulls. They were making a nuisance of themselves. It didn't help that people were throwing them fries. To their credit, they were better behaved than the gulls in Kelowna.

They did take a little ferry back downtown. It felt familiar to be back on the water. The fresh sea air—he didn't even smell the salt anymore. The crashing waves. The dip and dive of the boat. Patrick loved his job at the winery, but he knew he was going to miss being out on the water during the coming summer. It was going to be an adjustment. Good thing his boyfriend had a boat.

It took them a couple of hours to poke through the shops they had walked by the day before. Patrick ended up with a beanie hand-made by indigenous people in the Cowichan Valley. Charles, a box of expensive chocolates, and some cigars. Gifts for customers.

The sun had long since set by the time they pulled themselves away from their retail adventure which included a trip down Fan Tan Alley. A tiny alleyway between two sets of buildings with shops of umbrellas, metaphysical trinkets, and natural soap. Charles bought a few bars of shampoo.

Charles looked at his phone. "We have a dinner reservation in five minutes." He wrapped his arm around Patrick's shoulders. "It's just down this alley."

"Victoria has a lot of hidden alleys."

"That it does. We should go on a ghost tour. Find out what spirits linger in them." Charles laughed when Patrick stopped in his tracks.

"Not going to happen."

"You afraid of ghosts?" Charles kissed Patrick's head. "Now, I know something new about you." Charles stomped his foot on the ground. "See these cobbles—they're wood."

Patrick looked down at the ground. Charles was right.

"That's crazy."

"And it leads us to where we're going. The restaurant is right here."

Strings of white lights and shrubbery led you from the alley to a rather expensive-looking restaurant. Off a damned alley. It was a strange city with all sorts of nooks and crannies.

Inside, high ceilings, brick walls, and colorful original works of art. The hostess led them over to a table for two in front of a gas fireplace. It was cozy and somewhat private.

"This is nice," Patrick said.

"You're going to be blown away. They're known for their pasta."

"That is something I can totally get behind."

The meal they had was incredible and they paired it with local wine. Patrick hadn't realized there were so many wineries on the island. They were on their second bottle when Charles pushed his chair back, stood, and walked to the side of the table. His hands were shaking.

Patrick set his napkin back on his lap when Charles sunk onto one knee. His heart leaped and thundered in the chest. What the hell was Charles doing?

"Charles … what are you doing?"

Charles cleared his throat.

"Patrick, you have made me whole, and I'll never be able to repay you."

"You don't have to." Patrick pulled at Charles' sleeve. "Get up." He couldn't believe this was happening. It must have been the reason for the trip. Charles had been planning this all along.

Charles took one of Patrick's hands in his. "I want you to marry me."

Patrick looked around. People were watching … and waiting. If he could find a hole to escape into, he would. "Charles, I'm serious … get up," he whispered.

The word *forever* danced in his head. He'd said it to Charles. He'd said it and he'd meant it—at the time. Now, he wasn't so sure. Marriage—that was a huge commitment.

He wasn't ready.

He'd imagined them living together for months—maybe years before going down this road. He wanted to be sure. Did they truly have the connection needed to make it to forever?

Charles struggled back into his chair. "I thought …"

Patrick wasn't sure how to put it in words. "It's too soon."

That's the best he could do.

"Patrick, I love you." Charles held Patrick's hand in both of his. "I want to start a life together with you as my husband. Start a family."

Whoa. Backup.

A family?

They hadn't even talked marriage.

"We haven't talked about whether we want to have kids someday. With anyone. How do you know I even want any?" Charles was making a huge assumption. Sure, it was true, he wanted kids. But that was a talk you should have before a marriage proposal.

He was gradually becoming pissed at Charles.

They should have talked this through. Decided together. Not have Charles get down on one knee and throw a proposal at him in a public place. People had stopped looking but his ears were burning, he was so embarrassed. He pushed out his chair and headed for the door.

"Patrick, stop … I'm sorry."

It was the last thing Patrick heard before he took off outside and hailed a cab.

Chapter Eighteen | Charles

Charles slumped back in his chair. He signaled the server to bring him the check. He'd fucked everything up. Ruined it—brought it to a crashing end. With six little words.

I want you to marry me.

He would have liked to say the marriage proposal had been spontaneous, but it had been rattling around his head since before he booked the whole trip.

His nerves had been plaguing him all weekend. He'd convinced himself that Patrick was in the same headspace as him. That his proposal would be a romantic gesture that would be accepted without question. Patrick's reaction had floored him. It made him question everything. Their connection. Their compatibility—their love. Charles threw a pile of cash on the table.

As suspected, Patrick's luggage was gone by the time Charles stepped back into their hotel room. Charles had gone for a walk. Given Patrick a few minutes to clear out.

He sat on the bed.

His body shook as he wept. He rolled and lay down, his head on the pillow Patrick had been using. He trembled into the scent. The smell of his conditioner was still faint on the material.

He wasn't sure what to do next. Leave—or stay. He didn't want to be on the same flight as Patrick. That would make things even more awkward.

Stay until tomorrow.

Back for Tuesday night in the vineyard, picking the crop for ice wine. Charles held his hand on his face, shielding his eyes from the world. There was no way Patrick would be there.

He was alone.

He'd done this. Pushed too hard.

He convulsed through steady waves of grief—sobbing. The pillow was damp beneath his cheek. His world had been torn apart—again. He wasn't sure if Patrick would ever forgive him.

His life may as well be over.

He curled up and let his emotions overtake him.

His first day back at work—Tuesday morning, Patrick didn't show up for his shift. Charles found an email in his inbox. Patrick's notice. He wouldn't be coming back to the winery.

Charles spent the rest of the day in his office.

That night and for the next few nights, Charles was glad of the physical labor. Clippers in hand, gathering bunches of frozen grapes from the vines. Filling box after box. Pushing the next box along the frozen soil, the cold wind threatening to get under his warm clothing.

When he was done on the final night, he headed home. He dropped onto the sofa. He needed to talk to someone. His depression was getting the better of him.

He pulled out his phone.

Charles: "You up?"

Bianca: "Nope. Up 4 U though. What's up?"

Charles: "Put my heart out there."

Bianca: "What happened?"

Charles: "He broke it. My fault this time."

Bianca: "Why your fault?"

Charles: "Asked him to marry me."

Bianca: "Hold up. Last summer, you were single."

Charles: "It was quick."

Charles groaned when his phone rang.

Bianca.

"I don't know if I can talk about him," Charles said to Bianca.

"Tell me how you got there."

"He got under my skin. I fell in love. I so badly wanted him to be my husband."

"That goes without saying. Who is this guy?"

Charles took a deep breath. "Patrick. Aubrey's ex."

"The guy you hate?"

"That wore off. Turns out neither of us is a creature from the deep."

"O—kay. So, you started dating Aubrey's ex-boyfriend. Dated—had sex. The whole somewhat sordid and bizarre relationship. And you fell in love?"

"Yes, Bianca. I did—we did."

"I'm not even going to ask how that got started. So, you proposed to him, and he ran."

"Yes."

"You're sure he loves you?"

"Yes."

"So … what are you going to do about it?"

"What do you mean?"

"You're just going to let him go?"

"He's done with me. He even quit his job at the winery."

"Bullshit … complete and utter bullshit."

Bianca obviously didn't understand. Patrick had completely ghosted him. His reply to Patrick's email remained unanswered. Patrick didn't answer his calls or return his text messages.

"He doesn't want to talk to me."

"Let me tell you a little something about love, my dear. It doesn't suddenly disappear. He still loves you. You're still in love with each other. I'd say, that's a pretty good starting point."

"I don't know …"

"Charles. Smarten up. Don't you dare let him go."

Charles thanked Bianca and ended the call.

Still in love.

She was right. They had so much more than so many other people. They'd experienced love in their lives. Love for one another. That was no small thing.

They had promised each other forever.

He needed to hold onto that.

Charles grabbed his keys and headed for his car.

Chapter Nineteen | Patrick

Patrick lay on his bed, rolled up in the fetal position. He'd barely moved in three days. His life had collapsed around him. He'd fallen in love. And an obstacle had been thrown in his path. Marriage. Such a simple word for such a complex commitment.

He shifted his hip to move it off the mattress spring that was digging into him. He had a little over a week until he had to move out of his apartment. Where he was going to go, he had no idea.

He had no job. No money. Nowhere to live.

None of his friends would want a couch surfer.

He looked at his phone. He hadn't been able to pay his last bill.

It was dead.

He threw it onto the floor. If his mom hadn't sent him money for the plane ticket, he would have been stranded in Victoria.

Last week had been so full of promise. A man he loved was waiting for him to move in with him. To start a life together. They had promised each other forever.

Why had that changed?

Patrick ran his hands through his long, messy hair. Marriage was a big deal. It really was a promise of forever. Why was he so afraid of that? He loved Charles.

"He should have talked to me first," he said to no one.

That was the issue. Charles had sprung it on him without

consulting him. He'd made some huge assumptions. This wasn't the 1800s. He wasn't sitting around waiting for a proposal from the first eligible bachelor. Patrick sighed. It was his ego that had taken a hit.

And he'd blown his life up over it.

Fuck.

Patrick sat up, looked down at his phone, and pitched his pillow at it. He needed to hear Charles' voice. Have him tell him everything was going to be okay. That he was there for him.

He loved Charles more than his instinct to draw his next breath.

What the fuck have I done?

He nearly fell off his bed when someone pounded on his door. He tried to ignore it, but the knocker was insistent. He stumbled toward it and threw it open.

"What?"

Two calloused hands were immediately on his face. The kiss nearly took his knees out. He wrapped his arms around Charles' neck and held on as if his life depended on its existence.

Because it did.

He never wanted to be without Charles ever again.

His reservations melted away.

He broke the kiss.

"Yes … I'll marry you," Patrick whispered.

Charles pressed his forehead to Patrick's. "Are you absolutely sure?"

Sure.

He was more than sure. His soul had never wanted anything more than this.

"Marriage—kids. The whole thing. I want it all with you,"

he said.

Charles shuddered through a sob. "You're the most precious thing in my life."

"I can't live without you. I'm so sorry I ran."

Patrick gripped Charles' face and kissed him. It was filled with passion and commitment, and a need for one another. A need for a lifetime together.

The intensity of it—he could barely breathe.

Charles tipped his face away. He surveyed the space at the end of the entry hallway. "How do we get you out of here?"

Patrick turned and looked at his apartment. "I still have to clean it."

"What if we wrote off the damage deposit? Walked away. Hell … burned the whole damned place to the ground. I don't care. I just want you home."

"I wouldn't feel good about that. Leaving it a mess."

"Cleaners?"

Patrick sighed. "Sure." He couldn't stand to be there for a moment longer. He went back into the apartment and grabbed his phone, and a massive teddy bear there was no way he was leaving behind. He reached for Charles' hand. "Take me home."

The teddy took up most of the backseat of Charles' Range Rover. It made Patrick smile. Charles kept looking in his rear-view mirror at it. Before long, they were pulling into the driveway of their home. It looked different—the house. It was where he belonged.

Once inside, Patrick tossed the teddy onto the sofa.

Charles stepped in close to Patrick. "Welcome home." He cupped Patrick's face and kissed him—sensuous and deep. As always, the connection took Patrick to another place.

The sun rose in the background and lit up the living room.

The similarity was not lost on Patrick. Their relationship was entering a new level—a new day.

Charles took a step back and drew his finger up Patrick's throat to his chin.

"You have too many clothes on," he said.

"That can be rectified." Patrick lifted his shirt off over his head and tossed it to one side. He was slow to remove his pants. He was distracted by Charles doing the same. Soon, they stood naked before each other. Patrick breathed in the moment.

They had nothing to hide from one another.

They moved toward each other, slow and tentative. The rush of emotion that came with the next kiss had them both trembling. Hands traveled gentle—tender. Sighs and gasps as they reunited and restored the bond between them. Patrick pressed his hand against Charles' chest.

"Ask me again," Patrick said.

He needed to hear it again. To be sure it had really happened.

Charles sunk onto one knee and held Patrick's hand.

"Patrick, will you marry me?"

Patrick dropped to his knees and stroked Charles' face as he gazed into his eyes. Those beautiful brown eyes held his entire future in them. "A thousand times over."

A single tear escaped down Charles' cheek.

Patrick rose to his feet and drew Charles toward the sofa. He sat on it and prompted Charles to dig around in the basket they kept under the coffee table with the lube in it.

Every move that man made, was pure magnificence.

Charles took his time slicking up Patrick's cock. Patrick was groaning and desperate by the time Charles climbed onto the sofa and straddled Patrick's hips.

Patrick gripped Charles' hips as Charles guided him in. He

closed his eyes as Charles sunk fully onto him. He stroked Charles' skin from his hips up to his chest. Up onto his shoulders. Down his arms. Charles held steady the whole time, both enjoying the moment of simply being joined.

"I love you," Patrick said.

"I'll never stop."

Charles rose, then descended. He placed his hands on Patrick's shoulders. Rock—thrust—retreat. Again, and again. Their mouths sought each other out. Hot breath mingling.

Tongues—warm and wet.

Rise—and fall.

Charles grunted and spilled between them. He altered his pace. Slow—then fast. His powerful thighs carried him up and down. He leaned forward and breathed against Patrick's neck.

"Forever," he said.

Patrick held Charles' face steady and looked into his eyes.

"An eternity in your arms."

He spoke the truth. He'd never leave this man. They'd have each other; always. They'd have many children—a family together. And grow old, knowing they'd been destined to meet.

The joke was on Aubrey.

Hate to love. They'd taken that journey together.

Charles was his forever love—plain and simple.

Epilogue

Patrick and Charles stood at the front of the church together, hands linked. Charles had spoken his vows after Patrick. Charles' words had been serious, and loving, and he'd shared moments of devotion and commitment that they had experienced since their engagement. Patrick had been more light-hearted, joking about how they had come to end up dating each other. And how their hatred for each other had evolved and morphed into an intense love for one another.

The ceremony was beautiful. Most of the church was filled with Patrick's friends and family. Charles' side was slim but enthusiastic. Nearly everyone from the winery was there.

Their dog Merlot had been the ring bearer. He'd been adorable. Two months after they decided to be married, they'd adopted a black Labrador. The start of their family.

"You may kiss your husband."

The kiss was brief but meaningful. This was a new level in their life together. They had decided to wait a couple of years before they brought kids into the mix. They wanted to spend more time enjoying each other before they introduced some much-welcome distractions.

They walked back down the aisle together, hand-in-hand.

Bianca had already agreed to be their egg donor and surrogate. They joked about how they better prepare themselves for the possibility that one of their children might be a singer. How the sound of their voice would fill the large house. But for now, just them was enough.

Charles leaned close to Patrick. "We did it."

"That we did." Patrick smiled.

"Husband."

"Husband."

"On to the next adventure," Charles said.

Patrick gripped Charles' arm. "With you—anywhere."

Dear Reader

I hope you enjoyed reading *Merlot Rebellion*.

Please take a moment to review this book on the website of the store where you purchased your copy of *Merlot Rebellion*.

If you would like to touch base and say hello to the author, you can email them at: leigh@leighjarrett.com

About the Author

Leigh Jarrett (she/he) is an unabashedly queer, quirky, and passionate author of Contemporary MM+ Romantic Fiction. Their published contemporary works include warm and always sexy HEA romances as well as dark romances filled with grit, trauma, and angst.

In their hometown of Victoria, BC, Canada, Leigh can be found nestled up with their fabulously supportive wife and trusty laptop or enjoying the wondrous Vancouver Island outdoors.

Please consider subscribing to Leigh's newsletter to stay up to date with their new releases and promos. If you're interested in MM+ Fantasy and Paranormal Romance, check out one of Leigh's other pen names, JT Fader, on their JT Fader Fantasticals website and newsletter jtfader.com.

To connect with Leigh Jarrett:

Email: leigh@leighjarrett.com

Website and newsletter: leighjarrett.com

You can also find Leigh on Bluesky

Other Books by Leigh Jarrett

"It all came down to a matter of trust."
A Friends to Lovers M/M Gay Romance
Snowblind

"Risking it all to follow your heart."
A Found Family M/M Bisexual Romance

Capital Adoration

"Brave enough to pursue love."
An Age Gap M/M Gay Romance

Pacific Pursuit

"Learning a new path to love."
A Roommates to Lovers Bisexual Awakening M/M Romance

Academic Adoration

"Recovering true love."
A Second Chance Hurt/Comfort M/M Romance

Drag Undivided

"Strumming your way to love."
A Grumpy/Sunshine Gay Awakening M/M Romance

Rhythmic Bliss

www.ingramcontent.com/pod-product-compliance
Lightning Source LLC
Chambersburg PA
CBHW021039130626
46552CB00005B/1921

* 9 7 8 1 9 9 8 0 0 8 0 4 9 *